My Deadly Valentine

David W. Robinson

Copyright © 2013 by David W. Robinson
Photography: spekulator
Artwork: Crooked Cat
All rights reserved.

My Deadly Valentine: 978-1-908910-72-1
No part of this book may be used or reproduced in any manner whatsoever without written permission of the author or Crooked Cat Publishing except for brief quotations used for promotion or in reviews. This is a work of fiction. Names, characters, places, and incidents are used fictitiously. Any resemblance to actual persons living or dead, business establishments, events, or locales, is entirely coincidental.

Printed for Crooked Cat by Createspace

First Black Line Edition, Crooked Cat Publishing Ltd. 2013

Discover us online:
www.crookedcatpublishing.com

Join us on facebook:
www.facebook.com/crookedcatpublishing

The Author

A Yorkshireman by birth, David Robinson is a retired hypnotherapist and former adult education teacher, now living on the outskirts of Manchester with his wife and crazy Jack Russell called Joe (because he looks like a Joe).

A freelance writer for almost 30 years, he is extensively published, mainly on the web and in small press magazines. His first two novels were published in 2002 and are no longer available. His third novel, The Haunting at Melmerby Manor was published by Virtual Tales (USA) in 2007. He writes in a number of genres, including crime, sci-fi, horror and humour, and all his work has an element of mystery. His alter-ego, Flatcap, looks at the modern world from a cynical, 3rd age perspective, employing various levels of humour from subtle to sledgehammer.

A devout follower of Manchester United, when he is not writing, he enjoys photography, cryptic crosswords, and putting together slideshow trailers and podcast readings from his works.

David's online blog is at: **http://www.dwrob.com**

By the same author

The STAC Mystery series:

The Filey Connection

The I-Spy Murders

A Halloween Homicide

A Murder for Christmas

Murder at the Murder Mystery Weekend

My Deadly Valentine

Other work:

Voices

The Handshaker

My Deadly Valentine

A Sanford 3rd Age Club Mystery

David W Robinson

Prologue

A clutch of police cars, some with their blue lights still flickering in the fading, February twilight, stood outside 61 Carlton View. A uniformed officer ran yellow 'crime scene' tape across the bungalow's drive, while other officers stood by, holding back the inevitable crowd of nosy neighbours, and the press pack.

Inside the bungalow, officers from CID and Scientific Support went about their work with quiet efficiency, photographing the body and the setting, dusting for prints, examining every item of furniture and fittings for the slightest trace of anyone other than the victim. A doctor crouched over the woman, taking blood, while mortuary attendants stood by, waiting for the senior investigating officer to authorise the body's removal.

With a mixture of sadness and anger, Detective Sergeant Gemma Craddock of Sanford CID, looked down on the middle-aged woman. Laid on the bed, fully clothed, her bulging eyes staring up, skirt raised showing her stockings and sensible, department store underwear, a nylon coated washing line was wrapped tightly round her neck.

"Doc's already said she doesn't appear have been sexually assaulted, sir," she muttered. "Seems to me it's definitely the work of the Sanford Valentine Strangler."

"You should know better, Sergeant Craddock. Never assume anything," Chief Inspector Roy Vickers warned her.

He had been drafted in from Wakefield to head the investigation. A large, square-shouldered, no-nonsense man with over twenty years' service, he had an enviable arrest record, and Gemma had no doubt that he had seen much worse than this.

"Third year on the trot, Sergeant," he said. "Fiona Temple, two years ago, Thelma Warburton last year and now…" Vickers checked Gemma's notes. "Bridget Ackroyd."

"All on or around Valentine's Day, too," Gemma said. She picked up the card and paper flower next to it. "Same MO as the last two. Valentine card and paper flower on the mantelpiece." When she looked up to Vickers, her eyes were filled with pleading. "Sanford's a small town, sir. I don't think we've ever had a serial killer before."

"Precisely why I've been called in," Vickers reassured her. "No offence, but we're better equipped to handle them in Wakefield." He chewed his lip. "Trouble is, serial killers don't usually wait twelve months between murders. Normally it's a matter of a few weeks or months." With a sigh, he shrugged his overcoat tighter about his shoulders. "Where are you up to?"

"Usual stuff, sir. Our people are already talking to the neighbours and trying to trace any family. Like the others, she lived alone."

"Widowed?"

"Divorced, sir. We'll be checking the ex-husband, but the whisper is he's working away, somewhere."

He led the way out into the dark street where Gemma lit a cigarette and blew angry smoke into the coming night.

"The usual routine, sir?"

Vickers nodded. "You're already on with neighbours and family and you know the form. I want the full ABC of her movements over the last few days, and those of anyone close to her, anyone who could be considered a likely suspect. Check for connections between the dead women. Get it all logged, make sure you keep me up to date with all developments, not just those you consider important."

"Yes, sir."

Vickers looked down his nose at her. "And keep that bloody uncle of yours out of it."

Gemma smiled. "I think Uncle Joe is too busy with the Lazy Luncheonette and the Sanford 3rd Age Club."

Chapter One

"And don't burn the bloody toast this morning," one of the Sanford Brewery dray men grumbled.

Joe Murray took his money, rang it up in the till, and sorted out change. Handing it over, he glared. "How long have you been a dray man? Twenty years?"

"Give or take."

"Right. I don't tell you how to deliver barrels of beer, do I? So don't come in here telling me how to cook breakfast. Now bugger off so I can serve your mates."

The dray man wandered away chuntering to himself, and the next one arrived at the front of the queue. "Full English, Joe, and no toast. I'm not in the mood for your tantrums this morning."

Joe scribbled the order, passed it through the hatch to the kitchen, and poured tea. "If you or any of your mates don't like the service at the Lazy Luncheonette, go somewhere else."

The driver took his tea and handed over the money. "I'd miss the ambience, Joe, the pleasure of seeing your ugly mug every morning."

Seven thirty on a bitterly cold Monday morning in mid-February, and the Lazy Luncheonette was at its busiest. Many of the café's eighty seats were taken, a line of drivers, most of them brewery employees, queued almost back to the door where Joe had pinned up a large, handwritten notice reading, *WIPE YOUR FEET.* It was an attempt to keep the ice and snow of the outside world off the floor tiles where they would present a threat to staff and customers.

Sheila Riley, one of Joe's employees, and coincidentally, one of his best friends, had warned him it was too blunt. Joe, more liverish than usual, would not hear any criticism.

"It's not like I'm asking them to wear a collar and tie, is it? This is the Lazy Luncheonette, not the Ritz."

Outside, in the world men called real, the traffic backed up on Doncaster Road, the inclement weather exacerbated the usual morning jam and aggravated drivers' tempers. A turgid, leaden sky threatened more snow and chaos which were a part of a Great British winter. It could only get worse.

"Snow this late in February is usually gone in a day or two," Brenda Jump had said when it first appeared the previous Friday.

"So much for your weather forecasting," Joe had grumbled when she arrived for work this morning.

Brenda, his other best friend, doubled up as kitchen assistant to Lee, the cook, Joe's nephew. The system was tried and tested, and it worked. Behind the till, Joe whined and complained, while dishing out tea and taking money, Brenda and Lee prepared the meals, and Sheila could be seen dancing round the café delivering the orders. When he had a moment to spare, Joe would help her, and between them they cleared up the detritus of finished meals, passing the crockery back to the kitchen for washing up. It was hard work, but as a team they had it mastered and, when they got to the end of the day, even for grumpy Joe, there was satisfaction in a job well done.

The dray men of Sanford Breweries were his biggest and most loyal customers, perfectly at home with his irritation and outspoken rudeness, and they were often at pains to aggravate him further. It was almost as if his annoyance helped them cope with their own lives, persuading them that there really were others worse off than themselves.

"Think about it, Joe," Sheila had once said when in one of her teasing moods, "You serve as a horrible example and inspire other people to be better tempered and more polite than you."

"Polite," he had retorted, "doesn't get the job done."

If the weather outside was as irritable as Joe, the interior was kept warm by the crush of bodies feeding, and in the kitchen by the glow of ovens and hobs working at full capacity. But Joe's ire had an additional edge to it this morning, and Sheila was at a loss to understand why. And when she asked, she got short shrift.

"Just get on with feeding the five thousand," Joe snapped.

"He's narky because he hasn't got a date for Wednesday," Brenda called out from the kitchen.

The face on the driver Joe was serving split into a broad smile. "You're looking for a Valentine, Joe? Take my missus… please."

"One more word outta you and I'll call your missus and tell her what you get up to first thing on a morning."

"She won't care, as long as I'm not up to it with her."

"Just sod off," Joe said, handing over change. He turned on his staff. "And you lot, shut it and get on with what you're supposed to be doing."

With two full breakfasts and two bacon sandwiches perched precariously on her arm, Sheila danced past him. "At your age you should know better. You're behaving like a teenager."

"For your information, I am not in a bad mood because of Wednesday night."

"No. He's just in a worse mood than normal," Brenda called out. "Sheila, why don't you go as Joe's Valentine, and calm him down a bit?"

"I am not going as Joe's Valentine," Sheila replied haughtily. "Nothing personal, Joe, but I don't need a Valentine at all."

"So what's this Valentine thing all about, Joe?" asked the next dray man in the queue.

"The 3rd Age Club," Joe replied. "The barmpots wanted a night out for Valentine's, so we're booked into Churchill's, the big restaurant on Wakefield Road. Dinner and dance. Thirty quid a head."

"Churchill's eh?" asked the dray man. "Do they do a decent bacon butty there?"

Joe frowned. "I should think so. Why?"

"I was just thinking, I might get served a bit quicker if I went there for breakfast."

The frown wrinkling Joe's brow turned to a mean scowl. "Any more lip out of you and I'll throw you to Churchill's." He slammed a beaker of tea before the customer. "And you know where I'll shove the tea, don't you?"

***

Sat in the mess room, converted temporarily to a briefing room, Gemma had never felt so out of place in her own station.

All her uniformed colleagues were there, and so were the two CID men she supervised, but the rest were CID and Scientific Support officers from Wakefield and Leeds, brought in by Vickers to further the Sanford Valentine Strangler inquiry.

"All right, people, listen up," Vickers called out, bringing the briefing to order. "First off, two new faces for you. Des Kibble is our specialist dab man."

At the rear of the room a powerfully built, dark-haired officer stood up. His tanned features scowling, he nodded a greeting to the assembly.

"Des may be new to Sanford, but he's been with us a long time, and he's the best fingerprint officer in the business," Vickers went on. "He'll be going over the old case files to check on the fingerprint records and see if he can come up with anything new. The next new face is Paul Ingleton."

The lean-built, straw-haired man who stood up was a good deal taller than Kibble, and he smiled a friendly greeting at his new colleagues.

"Paul is our forensic photographer. Ex-army, been on the force about seven years, joined us from Bradford about five years ago and, like Des, he's the top man in his field. He, too, will be going over the old case files to see if he can highlight anything."

Vickers consulted his notes, then faced his team again. "In two days it will be Valentine's, Night. It's a year since the murder of Bridget Ackroyd, and we've made no progress. Whoever killed her, and the other two women in the years before Bridget, is still at large. So let's just remind ourselves of what we do know."

Vickers turned to the pictures on the wall, and pointed at the first, an enlarged image of a middle-aged, dark-haired woman.

"Fiona Temple. Aged fifty-one, divorcee. Lived alone in a terraced house on Leeds Road. Found dead in her bedroom on the morning of 15th February, three years ago. Her daughter-in-law had called on her, got no answer and became worried because Fiona had a heart problem, so she called the paramedics and ourselves. We broke in and found her laid on the bed. Her skirt was pushed up to the waist so her underwear was on view. However, post mortem revealed no sexual abuse. No sign of a struggle, nothing apparently missing from the house, purse intact, with about fifty pounds, plus cards, in it. Ligature was two bootlaces knotted together. They could have been bought from anywhere. There were traces of other people in the house, including family members, but nothing definitive, nothing that could lead us to a suspect. The shoe laces could have belonged to Fiona or the killer, we have no way of knowing, but Scientific Support speculated that she may have been killed elsewhere and her body brought home. Inquiry still open, but no action since last year, and still no clue to the killer's identity. Woman's husband returned from working in the Middle East a few months later, but he was never a suspect. He was in Dubai the night she died, and had been there for over a year. Alongside the bed we found a simple Valentine Card and a paper flower; a red rose. The card had a handwritten message which read 'Thank you, my love'. It was written in block capitals. We know the card could have been bought at any one of a dozen different outlets in Sanford, and hundreds of shops in Leeds or Wakefield. No forensic on the card at all."

Vickers moved on to the next photograph; a woman in her mid fifties, her hair white, features scowling into the camera.

"Victim number two. Thelma Warburton, aged fifty-six. Another divorcee. Her body was found on the morning of 19th February, the year before last, when neighbours became concerned after they hadn't seen her for several days. Post mortem estimated she had been dead for four days before she was discovered. Like Fiona, Thelma was found at her own home, on Willington Street. She was laid on her bed, fully clothed, but with her skirt pushed up to reveal her underwear. No sexual interference. The ligature was a length of twine, the stuff you can buy at the newsagents. Her family were not local, neither was her husband. Although she was born here in Sanford, she'd lived much of her life in Birmingham, moving back up here only after her divorce, five years prior to her death. Her two daughters and one son all live in the West Midlands, as does her ex-husband. All were accounted for on the night she died. Once again, there was little in the way of forensic, and once again we had a Valentine card with the same handwritten message as Fiona's. Analysis confirmed it was written by the same hand. This time the flower was purple."

Vickers moved on yet again.

"On 16th February last year, the third victim was found at her bungalow in Carlton View. Again, neighbours were worried about her. One of them looked through the back windows, saw Bridget and called us in. Exactly the same as the other two right down to her skirt pushed up, and the Valentine card with the handwritten message in the same block capitals, written by the same hand. This paper flower, like the first one, was red. Bridget was fifty-four and divorced. Ex-husband, an engineer of some kind, working in the Far East at the time of her death, and had been for three months. Forensic turned up a lot of evidence, most of it useless, yet again. Ligature this time was a washing line, the kind with a polymer covering, the kind you can buy anywhere."

Vickers turned from the board. "Three years, three murders and we've got nowhere. With forty-eight hours to go to Valentine's Night, we need the women of Sanford to be warned and vigilant. So our first task is to call on the pubs, clubs, bars, restaurants, cafes and get them to carry this poster on our behalf."

He held up an A4 sized poster, the headline written in bold, red capitals: *MURDER*.

Under the heading were three small images of the women and beneath that a warning in bold type.

These women were murdered on or about Valentine's Night. How well do you know your Valentine date? Take care. If you do not know your partner well, ensure you are not alone with him on or after the Valentine Night celebrations.

Vickers's stare took in all the men and women in the room. "Every pub, club, restaurant, shop and café in Sanford. Let's get to it."

***

Settling into table five, closest the counter, Joe drank from a beaker of sweet tea, and gazed blandly back in response to Brenda's glare. Alongside Brenda, Sheila smiled.

"I just thought if you asked her, it would save me a lot of problems," Joe said.

"You are not a teenager," Brenda retorted. "Ask the woman

yourself."

It was three thirty in the afternoon, and the Lazy Luncheonette was ready for closing. Lee had left at two, the cleaning was done, and the three remaining crew were settled for their customary last cup of tea of the day.

"Faint heart never won fair maid, Joe," Sheila pointed out.

"Cut the clichés," he retorted. "Come on, Brenda, you know me. I'm not good with women."

Sheila almost dropped her cup. "You didn't waste any time with Melanie Markham over New Year."

"She hit on me," Joe pointed out. "Aw, come on, Brenda, all I'm asking is that you ask Letty for a date on my behalf. Break the ice for me."

"I'll break a bit more than ice," Brenda threatened. "You never have a problem speaking to total strangers when they come in the café, do you? I've never heard such rudeness."

"That's business. And I don't think walking up to Letty and saying, 'you're a rough looking old sow, but you'll do for Valentine's Night', is gonna get me very far."

"She's not rough looking," Sheila pointed out. "In fact, she's quite pretty."

Joe took another mouthful of tea and sighed. "I didn't mean it literally. What I'm saying is I need to be a bit more tactful with her than I am with the customers, and me and tact are not always the best of friends."

"Tact and I," Sheila corrected him.

"Oh, I should say you're a lot more tactful than me, Sheila." Joe grinned at her.

She tutted and looked up at the ceiling as if seeking divine inspiration. She, too, drank from her beaker. "What is this sudden need for female companionship?"

Brenda guffawed. "Mid-life crisis... about fifteen years too late, I reckon. He's feeling his oats, isn't he? Ever since Melanie, he's been hankering after some more action."

"Not far off the mark," Joe agreed. "Look, I've been on my

own since Alison left, and that's, what? Ten years? Is there something wrong with wanting a woman in my life again?"

"Nothing," Brenda agreed. "Go for it, Joe, but go for it on your own, don't ask me to do your matchmaking."

"You have more experience than me, Brenda."

She stared sharply at him. "What?"

"You've had more men than Sanford Main Pit when it was running on three shifts, and…"

"You're walking dangerously close to the edge, Joe Murray. Be careful you don't fall off."

Sheila laughed. "Pushed, more like. Joe, how do you know Letty is even interested in men?"

Joe pointed at Brenda. "She told me so. When Letty first joined the club. Isn't that right, Brenda?"

"Well, yes, but she also said she's in no hurry."

"A widow, I believe," she said, and Brenda nodded.

"Her husband died very suddenly, about three or four years ago and she's been on her own ever since."

"No family?" Sheila asked.

Brenda shrugged. "A son in his thirties. Works for the European Commission and he's based in Brussels."

"A pen-pushing leech living on my VAT returns," Joe grumbled. "At least with me, she'd see a bit of life."

"The same way we do?" Brenda demanded. "From the wrong side of the Lazy Luncheonette counter?"

"Listen…"

The sound of the doorbell rattling, cut Joe off. A woman entered carrying a supermarket carrier bag. Her quilted anorak was buttoned up to the chin and the hood was raised against the sleet of the outside world.

"We're shut," Joe said from behind his beaker.

"Well open up again, it's the filth." Gemma threw back the hood of her quilted coat and grinned at them. "Hello, Uncle Joe, Mrs Riley, Mrs Jump."

They greeted her effusively, like an old friend they had not seen for a long time. Sheila took her coat and spread it over one of the radiators to dry off, Brenda moved behind the counter to make a beaker of tea for her, and Joe moved over to let his niece sit beside him. Dropping her carrier bag on the floor, Gemma reached in and came out with a bundle of posters wrapped in a transparent, polythene bag.

"Nice to see you again, Gemma," Joe enthused. "Just passing?"

"Official, I'm afraid, Uncle Joe." She removed one poster and handed it to him. "We're asking all businesses to pin up one of these."

Joe read it then passed it to Brenda. "The Valentine Strangler? I thought you nicked somebody for that after the last killing," he said while his two companions put their heads together to read the poster.

Gemma clucked. "Bloody newspapers. A few weeks after Bridget Ackroyd was killed we arrested and charged a man with rape and murders. He got it knocked down to manslaughter because he said he didn't mean to kill her. *The Sanford Gazette* and their resident terrier, Rosemary Ecclesfield, went bananas, insisting we'd nicked the Sanford Valentine Strangler. Truth is, we never said anything of the kind."

Joe smiled. "Don't let the truth get in the way of a good story, eh?"

"And how. There's a lot we don't tell the press, Uncle Joe, so they make it up as they go along."

Sheila passed the poster back to Joe, who reached over his shoulder to take a roll of tape from behind the cash register.

"You expect him to strike again the day after tomorrow?" Sheila asked.

"We don't expect anything, Mrs Riley, but we're taking no chances, hence the poster. I assume you two ladies will be out and about on Wednesday?"

"They're safe," Joe assured her. "The 3rd Age Club is going

to Churchill's for the evening and they have me to look after them."

"Ha!" Brenda's laugh dripped with cynicism. "Hark at him. A bodyguard he is not. He's too scared to ask Letty Hill for a date, never mind tackle a nasty strangler." She spoke to Gemma. "Anyone tries it with me, he'll get a good kick where he won't dare show his mum."

"Well, I have no need to worry, Gemma," Sheila said. "I shall be alone on Wednesday night, all night."

Brenda grinned. "That only leaves Joe for us to worry about."

"Bog off, you," Joe grunted. "Gemma, why didn't you call on your Uncle Joe sooner? I could have had this cracked long before now."

Gemma smiled. "Division have put Chief Inspector Vickers in charge of the case. Remember him, Uncle Joe? From the Wakefield jewel robbery inquiry the other Christmas?"

Joe frowned. "I remember him. He was glad of my help eventually."

"I believe he was, but one of his first orders to me, when he took over this case, was to keep you out of it."

"There's gratitude for you."

"Caution, I reckon, Joe," Brenda said. "You insulted him."

"Did I? I don't remember."

"As I recall, after he misread the word 'bark' as 'berk', you suggested Vickers should get himself a dog then look in a mirror so he'd be able to tell the difference."

Joe grinned. "Oh, yes. So I did."

Chapter Two

On Tuesday, from the moment Brenda delivered the news that Letty would be delighted to accept his invitation to accompany him at the Valentine dinner and dance, Joe spent much of the day in a spin. He calculated that it was his first proper date since before he married Alison.

"I'm outta practice," he told his companions when dithering about what he should wear.

"Even when you were in practice you were never the best," Brenda teased.

Passing much of the day in a daze, Joe had come down to earth by Wednesday morning, and after the lunchtime rush was over, he left the café for an hour, drove into town, and returned with a Valentine card and a single, red rose.

"I think I'd rather have grumpy Joe than a romantic Joe," Sheila had confided in Brenda as Joe preened himself before the mirror in the kitchen.

He locked up a few minutes early that afternoon, dealt with the books in record time, showered and shaved, and splashed on liberal helpings of an aftershave lotion, the name of which he could no longer read on the bottle. Making a mental note to buy new, he dressed in his dark blue suit, white shirt and a black bowtie, and at seven o'clock rang for a taxi.

For most STAC outings, Sanford Coach Services provided transport, but most STAC outings were to other towns and cities. With Churchill's sitting less than two miles from the town centre, it had been decided that the sixty members who had booked the Valentine's dinner and dance, would make their own way there. Joe had been tempted to drive, but common sense prevailed. It was rare that he went further than the Miner's Arms, and he knew he would be drinking.

It was impossible to miss Churchill's. Close to the motorway junction on Wakefield Road, a huge, neon sign in the shape of the wartime Prime Minister, complete with bowler hat and cigar, shone through the night. Despite its brash exterior, there was no compromise on quality. Churchill's official rating was four star but throughout Sanford it was known as the finest quality restaurant; *the* place to hold a celebration dinner.

Paying the taxi and getting out, Joe found a good number of his members already in the entrance and the air already resounded to their grumbles.

Captain Les Tanner, a former part-time soldier, looking militarily precise in his regimental blazer and tie, assumed the role of spokesperson. "About time, Murray. These dashed idiots won't let us in until you arrived with the official booking receipt." He waved irritably at the double doors of the entrance.

"And it's quite chilly out here, Joe," Tanner's lady-love, Sylvia Goodson added unnecessarily. Joe had already felt the cold when he got out of the taxi.

Dismissing their gripe, Joe pushed his way through the crowd, had a word with the maître, and a moment later, they began to file in, allocated tables as they entered.

Joe made his way to the back of the queue where he joined Sheila, Brenda and Letty.

"Sorry about that," he apologised to his date. "There are times when this lot are worse than a gang of schoolchildren."

"It's quite all right, Joe," Letty assured him. "Sheila and Brenda have kept me entertained, telling me tall stories about you."

Joe scowled at his grinning cohorts. "You don't wanna believe everything they say. They tell a lot of lies. Especially when I'm the topic of conversation."

Like Joe, Letty had gone to considerable effort with her appearance. Keeping makeup to a minimum, she wore a plain black dress, decorated with a pair of diamante brooches, both shaped like a young deer, and around her neck was a silver chain upon which hung a ruby pendant. At least, Joe assumed it was ruby. For all he really knew, it could have been red glass.

Feeling awkward, at a loss for something to say, he was saved by George Robson, who ranged himself alongside Brenda. Grinning gormlessly at Joe, George commented, "Nice dicky bow, Joe. Does it light up and spin round?"

"One of these days, George, someone is gonna use one of your spades to fill in your grave… and if you're not careful, it'll be before you're ready for it."

If Joe felt slightly ill-at-ease, he soon relaxed when they entered the building, and a waiter showed them to a discreet table for two off to one side of the dining area.

Most tables, he noticed, seated four, facing a small stage and dance floor. On the podium, a quartet of musicians was setting up their stands.

"The Ronaldo Lombardy Combo," Letty said with barely suppressed excitement.

Joe debated whether to tell her that Ronaldo Lombardy's real name was Ronnie Lund, and he'd been a trombonist with the Sanford Colliery Band before the pit shut down. In the end, Joe decided against saying anything. It was an evening for celebration, not nitpicking.

Across the aisle from them, making up a foursome, sat Brenda and George Robson, along with Sheila and Stewart Dalmer, a tall, rangy individual who had been a member of the club for about three years. A former tutor at Sanford Technical College, Dalmer was one of the more middle class members who rarely turned up at either meetings or on outings but, when he did, seemed to be in permanent opposition to the management trio of Joe, Sheila and Brenda.

The club members were spread about the vast, candlelit dining area, mingling with other patrons. Tanner and Sylvia were towards the back, sat with Alec and Julia Staines; Mavis Barker and Cyril Peck, as unlikely a pair as Joe had ever seen, were dining with Morton Norris and his wife.

He felt slightly embarrassed handing over the Valentine card and the single rose, but he need not have been. Letty was delighted.

After studying the picture on the front of the card, a couple arm in arm on a bench, watching the sun set over the ocean, Letty read aloud from inside. "I really need a valentine. How about it, kid? Joe." She beamed at him. "That's so nice, Joe. Thank you." At once, her features fell. "Oh dear. I didn't get you a card."

Joe smiled generously. "No worries. I didn't expect one." It was the truth. He had been more concerned that she might throw his back at him.

In the brief silence that followed, Letty looked around. "You must envy this place, Joe."

The observation puzzled Joe. The last thing he felt in regard to Churchill's was envy. "How so?" he asked.

"Well, you're in catering too. Would you not rather be running this place than your café?"

Under any other circumstances, the question would draw some forceful opinions from Joe, but he compelled himself to moderate his response.

"No, not really. See, these places are fine as they go. They turn out top notch meals, but look at the staff they need to cope with demand. We don't have that at the Lazy Luncheonette. Instead we have a bank of loyal customers who turn up daily, not just once a month or on special occasions. Because of that, I can plan better than these guys. If I were to break down the costs on a meal by meal basis, I reckon I'm on a better percentage."

"Very astute," Letty said. "My late husband, Brian, always

insisted that when it came to business, small and personal was best."

Joe accepted a menu from their waiter. "Yeah? He was a businessman, too?"

Letty nodded and studied her menu. "He had a small garage in Ferrybridge. Just off the A1. Repairs and secondhand car sales. He never aspired to anything bigger, but he employed two mechanics and made a good living." A wistful glaze came over her blue eyes. "Taken far too early."

"How old was he?" Joe asked, and promptly brought himself up short. "Sorry. I didn't mean to shove my nose in."

"I don't mind talking about it, Joe. He was just forty-nine. Heart trouble. He'd suffered from a weak heart since his childhood. I'd often warned him about the hours he kept and the hard work he put in." Letty sighed. "He jacked up one car too many and had a heart attack."

"I'm sorry," Joe repeated, more sincerely this time.

A wan smile played across her lips. "The pain fades, you know, but it never really goes away. I've been on my own for three years now, and I thought it was time to start getting out, I know Brian would not have wanted me to become a permanent, grieving widow."

With his natural, cautious conservatism, Joe chose a well done fillet steak, Letty agreed, and Joe ordered both, with a bottle of Cabernet Sauvignon to complement the meal. Both chose melon for starters and while they waited for the food, Letty asked, "So you know about Brian and me, what's your story?"

"Divorced," he said with a frown brought on by unpleasant memories. "Alison was a local lass. I knew her from schooldays. We married fairly late in life. I was thirty-five. She knew about the café long before we even started going steady, so she really had no excuse, but unlike you and your husband, she didn't see business for what it was; a big responsibility which takes up so much of your time. After ten years, she'd had enough and we split up. Then, five years ago, she flew off to Tenerife and never came back. She's still out there."

The wine waiter arrived, opened the bottle for them and offered Joe the cork. He declined. "I know less about wine than I do bottled beer, so just pour it, son."

Soon, sipping on the wine, working their way through the starter, Letty pressed him further.

"Did you feel betrayed, Joe? When Alison and you split up, I mean."

He shrugged. "Not really. Things were bad between us towards the end, but I can honestly say there was no other man – or woman – involved." He chewed on a tough piece of melon, wondered what to do with it, and swallowed it with a loud gulp. "Excuse me." He washed it down with a mouthful of wine. "That bit needed another few days to ripen." He beamed at her and allowed the smile to fade slowly. "I'm fifty-six now, and I'm getting to thinking I need a bit more from life than the Lazy Luncheonette. Don't misunderstand me, Letty. I'm in no rush. But I can leave Lee to take care of the café, while I allow myself a little more freedom."

Letty pushed her plate to one side, reached across and touched his fingertips. "That, Joe, is exactly how I feel."

Encouraged by this simple act, Joe loosened up, and the evening progressed, through the meal and dessert (Joe settled for fruit salad, Letty preferred strawberries and ice cream) and by the time they were on the coffee and brandies and Joe had excused himself to step outside for a smoke, he felt sufficiently emboldened to ask her to dance.

He had never considered himself a good dancer, but he was light enough on his feet to move Letty round the floor to the strains of The Carpenters' *We've Only Just Begun* coming from the trombone, keyboard, drums and guitar of Ronaldo's Combo.

As they moved along, his nostrils filled with the heady scent of her perfume, he noticed Brenda and George Robson smooching, and close to them, Sheila dancing with Stewart Dalmer. Although Dalmer was a better dancer, Joe consoled himself: the height disparity between him and Letty, a mere inch or two, was better than that between Dalmer's six feet four inches, and Sheila's five feet and a couple of inches.

"Sheila's letting her hair down a bit," Joe commented. "Don't normally see her dancing with strangers."

"Stewart?" Letty asked. "Nice man."

"You know him?"

"Slightly," she admitted with a blush. "He was interested in one or two antiques I own. He took me out to dinner a few times, but I made it clear that the pieces were not for sale."

The tempo changed; Ronaldo and his small band switched to Neil Diamond's *Sweet Caroline* and Joe escorted Letty back to their table.

"Sentimental value? Or genuine antiques?" he asked.

"Both, really. I have some Victorian china and a set or Regency silver spoons worth a tidy sum. But they were Brian's. Handed down through his family, and I won't part with them. When I go, they'll pass to Tim."

"Tim?"

"My son. He works for the European Commission."

Joe suppressed a vitriolic comment concerning Brussels. "Ah. I see."

As the evening drew on, they danced again, this time to a somewhat obvious *My Funny Valentine* and Matt Monro's *Portrait of My Love*, while sitting out the more upbeat numbers of The Stylistics *You Make Me Feel Brand New* and the (again) obvious *Unchained Melody*. The process of getting to know each other continued slowly, interrupted only occasionally when other club members, among them Sheila, Brenda, Les Tanner and Julia Staines, came to sit with them for a few minutes at a time. By eleven, when the party began to break up, Joe felt he had known her for most of his life instead of the last three and half hours.

Stepping out into the frosty, clear night, Joe was surprised to learn that Sheila, Brenda and George Robson had already left.

"They took a taxi together," Alec Staines told him. "That's one hell of a threesome if you think about it." He grinned drunkenly, drawing a glance of disapproval from his wife.

"They were dropping Sheila at home," Julia said, "and Brenda hinted that she and George were going on to a club in town."

Joe knew Brenda – and George – well enough to know that bed was a more likely option than a club.

He refrained from saying so, and asked Letty, "Where do you live?"

"Oakleigh Grove," she replied. "I can get a taxi, Joe. I'll be all right."

Her address was out of his way, but Joe asserted himself. "We'll share a cab. I'll get the driver to take you home, and when we've dropped you off, he can carry on to the Lazy Luncheonette."

Letty did not argue and ten minutes later they climbed into a cab, Joe wondering how far he was supposed to go on a first date. Was a goodnight kiss in order? Should he hold back and merely ask if he could see her again? Why hadn't he taken Brenda more seriously; if anyone could teach him the rules of dating, it was her.

The taxi wove its way through the streets of Sanford, from Churchill's location in the south, to Letty's home in the northeast, where, after working his way through a suburban maze of streets, the driver finally turned into Oakleigh Grove, a street of large, detached bungalows, and drew to a halt outside number thirty-three.

Joe studied the new-ish Fiat in the drive, the spread of winter-neglected lawn at the front, and the neatly trimmed dwarf conifers bordering the grass. "Nice place," Joe commented. He compared it to other houses on the street. All had that same air of middle class homogeneity. "Nice area."

"I like it, Joe. Brian liked it. We lived here since we first married." Hand on the car door, Letty prepared to get out.

"Listen, Letty, I wondered… er, I just… sort of…" Mentally, Joe cursed himself. Why was he so tongue-tied? It wasn't as if he was asking her to marry him or anything.

Hand still on the door, ready to get out, Letty waited expectantly. "Yes?"

"Well, I wondered if I could see you again." Joe was glad of the dark. It hid his blush.

She smiled and took his hand. "Why don't you pay the driver and come in for a cup of tea?"

Joe was taken completely by surprise. "Oh, er, yeah. Okay. Gimme a minute."

Letty climbed out while Joe fumbled for his wallet, paid the fare and climbed out.

"Good luck," said the driver.

Joe watched the tail lights disappear around a bend in the street. "Keep your phone on, pal," he muttered. "I'll be needing you again in half an hour."

Lights were coming on in the house as he walked up the path to the side, knocked politely on the open kitchen door and stepped in.

Letty was fussing over the kettle and tea tray. "No need to knock, Joe. Go through to the lounge and make yourself comfortable. I'll just make the tea."

Joe passed through the small kitchen and into the living room. It was immediately apparent that Letty was house proud. The mahogany coffee table gleamed from a coat of polish, the matching surround of the mock fireplace had an almost mirror finish to it, and even the out-of-date TV stood in the corner by the window, showed no trace of dust. In the opposite corner, behind a leather armchair, stood a tallboy containing a number of china figurines, some items of silver and photographs, mostly of Letty and another man.

"My husband," Letty said putting a vase on the lower shelves of the tallboy, and dropping the rose into it. She moved to the fireplace and stood Joe's card in the centre, blocking off a small clock with a mock-wood surround that matched the rest of her furniture. "I'll fetch the tea."

While she disappeared back into the kitchen, Joe studied the photographs more closely.

Brian Hill had been tall, lean, fit and athletic, and if Letty had not told him of the heart defect, Joe would have surmised he was the last man in the world to suffer such an ignominious death. The pictures had been taken when they were on holiday. Cornwall, Joe guessed, his judgement based on the rugged cliffs in the background. He had no clue how old the photographs were, but Letty looked happy and a good few years younger.

"Tintagel, at the millennium," Letty said coming back with the tea tray. "We loved the southwest."

"Long time since I was last down there," Joe replied, settling into one corner of the settee and helping himself to a cup of tea. "The club are going down that way for a week later this year. Perhaps you'd like to come. There are spaces on the bus."

"We'll see," Letty replied, making herself comfortable in the armchair.

Joe noticed how much more relaxed she was than he. Would he be just as relaxed if they were in his flat above the Lazy Luncheonette? He doubted it.

Putting down her cup, Letty reached behind to the tallboy and took down a dark blue, velvet case containing six teaspoons, and handed it to Joe. He had spotted it open on the shelf, but paid little attention.

"Remember you were asking about Stewart Dalmer? He offered me four hundred pounds for them."

Joe whistled. "And they're worth it?"

"Nearer five hundred," Letty replied. "They're silver,

naturally. They've been in Brian's family since Victoria was queen. They came via his grandfather and father. I wouldn't sell them for ten times their cash value."

Gingerly, Joe handed them back, as if he was afraid he might drop and break them. Groping through his thin fund of small talk, he commented, "You should make sure they're well insured."

"Already covered, Joe."

An uncomfortable silence fell. Letty appeared quite comfortable sipping her tea and Joe was at a loss for anything to say. Had he been this quiet when in his younger years.

"A good do, tonight," he said.

"A very good do," Letty concurred.

Another awkward silence fell. Joe wondered if Letty was interested in rugby league, but right away he dropped the idea. *He* wasn't sufficiently interested in rugby league to build a conversation on it.

He gulped down his tea. "Could I, er, use the smallest room?"

Letty nodded to the hall. "Turn left, and straight ahead." She smiled. "I don't charge."

Joe grinned. "Neither do I."

He had no need of the lavatory. He had simply been chasing some space, a few seconds away from the intense pressure of silence which he felt he was supposed to break.

Looking in the mirror, his crinkly hair and creased brow threw questions back at him. Was this the same man who was never lost for words when he stood behind the counter of the Lazy Luncheonette? Was this the man from whom insults, empty threats, witty, cutting rejoinders flowed so easily when the dray men of Sanford Breweries gave him cheek? Why, then, was he approaching Letty as if he was walking on eggshells?

He made up his mind there and then, flushed the lavatory to give the impression that he had actually used it, turn and marched out of the bathroom… only to bump into Letty right outside the door.

For a moment he wondered what she was doing there. Checking up to ensure he didn't steal the soap? Then she threw her arms around his neck and drew his lips to hers.

Joe's surprise melted and the kiss became filled with passion as he enfolded her in his arms.

Breaking her lips from his, Letty whispered, "It's been so long, I've almost forgotten what it feels like to snuggle up to man under the duvet."

Chapter Three

Averting her eyes from the body on the bed, Gemma took the diary from one of Vickers' detective constables, moved from the bedroom to the kitchen, sat down and, slipping on a pair of disposable, forensic gloves, opened it.

A pocket diary, the cover a pale pink decorated with white daisies, contained few entries, mostly appointments, but as she thumbed through it, Gemma was disturbed to find several damning entries.

January 20th: *Sheila Riley persuaded me to join the Sanford 3rd Age Club. My first STAC disco on Wednesday.*

January 24th: *Wonderful night last night. Joe is such a charming man. Not as grumpy as they make him out to be.*

January 31st. *The STAC is so much better than the internet dating sites.*

February 13th: *Good heavens! Brenda says Joe would like me to be his Valentine tomorrow night.*

February 15th: *Joe is so much more than a grumpy businessman. Naughty but nice.*

A frown etched itself into Gemma's clear brow. When the words Sanford 3rd Age Club and Joe came together, it could mean only one thing.

"Interesting reading, Sergeant?"

Startled, Gemma looked up to find Vickers stood over her. "Oh. Sorry, sir, didn't hear you come in. I wouldn't say interesting, but it's something we need to look into."

"Well, let's look at the victim, shall we?"

Gemma led him to the bedroom where he looked over

Letty's body, eyes open, staring sightlessly at the ceiling, fully clothed, her skirt pushed up to reveal her underwear, black cord still wrapped around her neck.

His face a mask of contemptuous disgust, Vickers asked, "Same MO as the others?"

"Yes, sir. Exactly the same. No sign that she had had sex. Simply strangled."

"And the neighbours saw and heard nothing?"

"We're out there asking them right now, sir."

Vickers concentrated on the doctor. "Time of death?"

"Difficult," the doctor replied. "Central heating was on when we got here. I'd guess she's been dead six to eight hours."

The chief inspector checked his watch. "Midnight-ish, then." He faced Gemma. "Robbery?"

"We're not sure. Doesn't look like it."

Vickers' gimlet eye fell on the diary. "All right, Sergeant, what was it you found so interesting in that diary?"

Without a word, Gemma handed the diary over, opened at the January 31st entry.

Vickers's eyes rose. "Your uncle?"

She nodded. "I know of no other Joe Murray in Sanford, and I know that Uncle Joe is Chair of the Sanford 3rd Age Club. Hardly likely to be a coincidence, but I know he had nothing to do with this."

"Let's not confuse what you believe with what you really know, Sergeant. You assume he had nothing to do with this. And if I hadn't shown up, what would you have done? Spoken to him in an effort to cut him out of the investigation?"

Gemma bristled. "I resent that, sir. I am a professional, not a probationer. I don't let personal considerations get in the way of my job. I would have followed procedure and passed it on to you."

"Unimpressed," Vickers retorted, "but I'll be charitable and believe you. Come on. Let me show you something."

He led her from the bedroom back to the lounge where

more forensic officers were at work. As they entered, one officer approached.

Vickers introduced the pair. "Des Kibble, this is Detective Sergeant Craddock. Craddock, Des Kibble. Dab man. You met at the briefing the other day. What is it, Des?"

"An opinion, guv," Kibble replied. "I shouldn't think it was robbery."

"No?"

Des waved at the tallboy. "Set of half a dozen silver spoons in a display case. Can't tell, offhand, but they look Regency. And on the top shelf, the shepherd is Capo di Monte." He gestured again, this time at the shepherd boy with a lamb around his neck, standing next to the glass vase containing a single red rose. "Those two alone are worth upwards of a grand."

For Gemma's benefit, Vickers explained, "Des is into porcelain and precious metals, aren't you, Des? Any prints on them?"

"No, sir. I checked her purse and that's untouched, too. Forty pounds in cash, and a bit of change, plus the usual plastic." Kibble grimaced. "This is not a robbery."

"I'll bear it in mind," Vickers said and dismissed Kibble with a curt nod. "Miserable git," he said as the dab man left.

"Sir?" Gemma asked.

"Transferred in from Bradford a few years back. He'd been involved with some woman when she just disappeared. No trace of her anywhere. No evidence of foul play, but tongues started wagging. You know how it is. He asked for a transfer and he's been with us ever since. He's also been like a bear with a sore arse ever since. Good at his job, though." Vickers brought his attention back to the crime scene, concentrating on the fireplace, where a Valentine card stood alongside an old photograph of Letty and her late husband. Beside the card was a paper flower, fabricated in yellow, this time. The card showed an image of a couple, almost in silhouette, arm in arm on a bench, watching the sun set over the sea. Emblazoned with a red heart, the caption read, '*Be My Sunny Valentine*'.

"What interests me isn't the card, but the signature," Vickers said, putting on forensic gloves and picking it up.

He handed it to Gemma and she read the spidery handwriting. *I really need a valentine. How about it, kid? Joe.* Further down, in block capitals was written, *Thank you, my love.*

"A departure from his previous killings. Do you recognise the handwriting?" the chief inspector asked.

"The line at the bottom looks just like the cards in other years," Gemma said with a sinking heart. "But the rest of it… Uncle Joe."

"I think it's time we paid your wicked uncle a visit."

***

Joe took everyone by surprise on Thursday morning by not showing up, leaving it to Lee, Sheila and Brenda to open up. He rang at 7.15am and told them he would not be in until Friday morning.

"The first time in living memory Joe has taken a day off," Sheila commented as she battled with the morning queue of delivery drivers.

It was a losing battle and by eight they had to ring for Cheryl, Lee's wife, to come in and lend a hand.

When Joe showed his face again, on Friday morning, he came under immediate fire from both his companions, yet remained stone faced, grouchy and uncommunicative on the subject of Letty.

"Whatever happened is between me and her," he told them. "Now let's get on with it. We have people waiting to eat."

The driver waiting to order his breakfast concurred. "If the bloke in the paper shop next door asks how I am, tell him I'm famished."

Joe pushed a mug of tea at him. "If you're going to starve to death, do it outside. That way I don't get Environmental Health breathing down my neck."

He had spent Wednesday night with Letty. Most of the time he was in a state of amazement that such a demure and outwardly modest character could be so demanding in the dark of the bedroom.

"Even if I wanted to go to work, I don't think I'd have the energy," he told her on Thursday morning.

He stayed with Letty up until lunchtime, when they agreed to a night out in Leeds over the weekend. From there he took a taxi into Sanford and killed off three hours wandering around the shops, and picking up brochures from several travel agencies. He sneaked back into the Lazy Luncheonette just after four, having watched Brenda lock up a few minutes earlier, and spent the evening going through the brochures.

"If me and Letty are gonna get it together, why not take in a bit of sun," he muttered as he pored over photographs from Mediterranean resorts.

Through the Friday morning rush, Brenda pestered him, but he remained tight-lipped. At ten thirty, with the rush over, while Lee prepared lunches, Joe, Sheila and Brenda took their break at table five, in front of and to the right of the counter. With only one or two shoppers in, Brenda took the opportunity to badger Joe on the events of Wednesday night and most of Thursday.

"I want all the dirty details," she said.

"Nothing happened," he assured her.

"Not good enough, Joe Murray. You didn't show your face here yesterday, and we know you. If you were home on Wednesday night, you wouldn't take the morning off, never mind all day."

"You wouldn't take an hour off," Sheila declared.

"Which means you didn't come home on Wednesday, you dirty stop out. Now come on, Joe. What sort of knickers does she wear, or did you have the lights out."

Joe drank his tea and basked in the warmth of his memories and the greed for information. "If I knew, do you think I'd tell you? I've told you before, I'm not the kind to kiss and tell."

"And I'm not asking about the kissing," Brenda pressed. "I'm interested in the…"

"I think that's enough, Brenda," Sheila interrupted. "Joe is entitled to some secrets. Aren't you, dear?"

"Course I am. What I will tell you is I'll be seeing Letty again on Saturday night."

Brenda's face lit up. "At the Miner's Arms? I can nag her to tell me how good you are, in that case."

"Not at the Miner's Arms," Joe retorted. "Why the hell would I take a classy lady like Letty Hill to the Miner's Arms on a Saturday night? We're thinking of going through to Leeds for a film and meal after."

Brenda chuckled. "Last Tango in Pontefract?"

Sheila, too, tittered. "Belle de Dewsbury?"

"You can laugh." Joe took out his tobacco tin and prepared a cigarette. "Anyway, how did you get on after Churchill's?"

"Brenda and George Robson took me home in their taxi," Sheila said, "and I went straight to bed… alone, of course. As I prefer it."

"Then George and I went back to his place and I showed him how to tidy up."

Joe grinned. "I'll bet that took all night, too." He yawned. "Better go for a smoke before the lunchtime rush. It's enough leaving you lot in charge for a whole day. I'll not make a habit of it."

Sheila scowled at him. "We can cope, Joe. We won't bankrupt you. We're not dangerous, or anything."

The clatter of pans and at least two plates hitting the kitchen floor, reached their ears, followed by Lee's cry of, "Aw, jiminy."

"I wish he'd learn to swear like a proper Yorkshireman." Joe stared at the two women. "You were saying?"

"That's Lee," Sheila reminded him. "He's like that even when you're here, and it's clumsiness, not dangerous. When it comes to running this café, Joe, you're the best. When it comes to managing your staff – us – you're the absolute pits. You never learned how to delegate."

"When you're not here…" Brenda began, only to be cut off by the doorbell, and the entry of Gemma and Chief Inspector Vickers.

Joe greeted them with a smile of relief. "Hello, Gemma. And look who it isn't. How are you, Vickers? Want some tea?" he rose from his seat.

Grim-faced, Vickers said nothing but nodded to Gemma.

"No thanks, Uncle Joe. We want to ask you a few questions. Well, one question really."

Puzzled, Joe invited, "Ask away."

"Do you know a woman named Letitia Hill?

Joe let out an irritable sigh. "Why can't everyone mind their own business when it comes to me and Letty? What about her?"

In deference to the two women present, Gemma retreated slightly. "Can you tell us where you were last night between, say, ten o'clock and three this morning?"

Joe's grumpiness turned to full blown suspicion. "At ten, I was in front of the TV watching the news. By half past eleven I was in bed, where I stayed until about five this morning."

Gemma looked to her superior, and it occurred to Joe just how uncomfortable his niece appeared. She looked as if she wanted Vickers to take over.

Vickers did not. Instead, he nodded to Gemma again.

"I'm sorry, Uncle Joe, but you'll have to come with us to the station."

"Like hell. I have a business to run here."

"You either come with us, Murray, or you'll be arrested,"

Vickers assured him.

Joe rose to the challenge. "On what charge?"

"No charge, merely suspicion."

"Of what?"

"Murder."

Joe's jaw dropped and the colour drained from his tanned face. Sheila and Brenda snapped their heads round to face the chief inspector, and even Lee appeared in the kitchen doorway.

"What?"

"Letty Hill was found dead at her bungalow, this morning," Gemma said. "She'd been strangled."

Joe flopped into his seat opposite Sheila and Brenda. "I... er... Oh, bloody hell."

"We need to speak to you, Uncle Joe, if only to eliminate you from our inquiries."

Joe responded only sluggishly to his niece. "What? Oh. Yes. Obviously. Of course you do." He shook his head vigorously, clearing his mind, concentrating his wits. "But surely you can speak to me here?"

"It's a formal interview, Murray," Vickers replied. "It will be recorded. We'll need fingerprints and a DNA sample for comparison purposes. It has to be done at the station."

Joe glowered. "Sod off, Vickers. You know damn well I didn't kill her."

"There is a difference between what I may know intellectually and what I know for a fact," the chief inspector retorted. "My superiors and the courts will not take my opinions or my knowledge of you into account. Now, you either come with us voluntarily, or I will insist that Sergeant Craddock arrest you. And I don't care whether she's your niece or not. It's your choice."

Sheila again reached across the table and took Joe's hand. "You're obviously upset, Joe, but you should go with them. Would you like one of us to come along?"

Joe shook his head. "I need you two to run the café while I

tear them to pieces." Heaving in a deep breath, he stood up. "One condition, Vickers. I come in my own car. I'm not forking out for a taxi back from Gale Street."

Vickers smirked in triumph. "As long as you don't try to do a runner."

***

Joe was perfectly accustomed to the small, cramped interview rooms at Sanford Police Station, or any police station, come to that, but in the past he had sat on the other side of the table, with the police, helping them with their inquiries.

But once the police had taken his fingerprints and allowed a DNA swab, he found it disconcerting to face Vickers and Gemma in the tiny room while they announced themselves to the recording devices.

On the ten minute drive from Doncaster Road, his thoughts had been centred around Letty, their evening out on Wednesday, and its aftermath.

Joe was too old to believe in love at first sight, but their relationship had got off to the most promising of starts. Now it was not to be, and Joe, for all that he had only known her for a few days, took it personally.

Parking his car on the multi-storey in Sanford High Street, he had made his way quickly through the crowds of shoppers into the backstreets and arrived at the redbrick, late nineteenth-century Police Station only a few minutes after Vickers and Gemma, from where they had hustled him through to the interview room. His mind was burdened with questions and he knew he would get no answers until Vickers was satisfied that Joe had successfully accounted for himself.

And yet he had not rehearsed any responses, as the police discovered when, after he had identified himself to the recording device, and refused legal counsel, they repeated the questions he had been asked back at the Lazy Luncheonette, and they moved onto deeper inquiries.

"How long had you known Mrs Hill, Mr Murray?" Gemma asked, maintaining a formality as uncomfortable for her as it was irritating for Joe.

"I met her at the end of January, when she joined the 3rd Age Club. Sheila knew her – slightly – and canvassed her to join the club."

Vickers had Letty's diary open in front of him. "We did note that you'd only known her a couple of weeks when you asked her for a date on Valentine's Night. Did you think it a little odd when she accepted?"

"Not especially. I met her, I liked her, I found the bottle to ask – well, to be honest, Brenda found the bottle to ask on my behalf, and Letty accepted. It's not so odd when you think about it. At our age, you don't want to be hanging around too long."

"Not like you to be dating women, is it?" Gemma asked.

"What do you think I'm made of, girl? I've been on my own for ten years now. Ever since your Aunt Alison and I split up. I may be no Romeo, but I'm not completely…"

Joe trailed off as Vickers reached across to the recorder.

"This recording paused at…" Vickers interrupted, checking his watch, "… Eleven thirty one." He paused the machines. "Sergeant Craddock, I'd like you to leave and send in Constable Brooks to take your place." He eyed Joe. "Your uncle has just identified you as his niece."

Joe fumed. "Will you get the pole out of your backside, Vickers? You know damn well I had nothing to do with Letty's murder, so this is no more than a bloody formality."

Gathering her belongings, Gemma explained, "There are procedures, Uncle Joe…"

"I don't give a bugger about your procedures. While you are wasting my time, you're also leaving the real killer out there, free to murder some other poor woman. Now for God's sake, sit down and let's get on with it."

Both officers were taken aback with his vehemence.

"I realise this situation is unnerving for you, Murray—" Vickers began, only to be cut off by Joe.

"I am not nervous. I'm bloody annoyed. Letty and I had had one date and we'd planned a second. We were in the process of getting to know each other and now she's dead and it's getting to me because I'll never get to know her properly."

It seemed to Joe that most of his words went over Vickers's head. "Getting to know her. After just one date?"

"Yes? And?"

"Would you repeat that on tape?"

Joe let out a frustrated sigh. "There you go again. For the last time, I did not kill her. And I'll repeat everything in open court if it'll make you get your finger out and look for the real killer."

Vickers reached for the recording machine again with the instruction, "Try not to identify Sergeant Craddock as your niece again."

With the machine running, Vickers asked the pertinent questions and Joe told them of the evening out at Churchill's.

"Did you go to Mrs Hill's last night with the intention of pressing her for another date?" the chief inspector asked at length.

"That's a leading question or I never heard one," Joe complained. "If I say, 'no', you might well ask why did I go there, then. So let me make it clear. I did not go anywhere near Letty's place last night. I haven't seen her since I left, about one o'clock yesterday. And we had already planned to meet again on Saturday."

"But you have been to the bungalow before, Mr Murray?" Gemma asked.

"Yes. I spent the night there on Wednesday."

"So we will find traces of you in there?"

"I should think so."

Vickers frowned. "Why did you stay the night?"

Joe fumed. "Because she wanted me to paper the hall ceiling. Why do you think I stayed, you idiot? She invited me."

"You pressured her."

Joe shook his head and then remembered the recording. "No I did not. In fact, I was about to let her get out of the taxi when she asked me in for coffee. Half an hour after that, I was about to leave, when she practically dragged me into her bed. Now what the hell do you take me for, Vickers?"

"You don't want to know the answer to that." Vickers produced the Valentine card and laid it on the table. Allowing Joe to study the front, he then opened it while Gemma reported the actions for the benefit of the recording. "Do you recognise this?"

"Yes." Joe made no move to pick it up. "I bought it for Letty on Sanford market on Wednesday afternoon."

"And you wrote the greeting on the inside?"

"Yes." Joe aimed a bony finger at the bottom line. "I didn't write that, though. It's not even in the same colour pen I used."

"We'd noticed. When did you give her the card?"

"Wednesday. At Churchill's."

"When did you give her the paper flower?"

Joe's brow knitted. "What paper flower?"

Gemma produced the yellow paper flower. "This was on the mantelpiece, next to the card, Mr Murray." Gemma explained.

Joe shook his head. "Nothing to do with me. I gave her a *real* flower. A red rose. And I gave her that in Churchill's, too. Are you really this gormless, Vickers? Didn't you take my advice from Wakefield when I told you to find a bit on the side?"

"Now listen—"

"I just said, I gave her the card and a red rose while we were at Churchill's and that is all. We were there for Valentine's Day. What did you think I'd do? Send her a bill for the restaurant? She put the damn thing on her fireplace, and stuck the flower in a vase, but there was no paper flower when I left." He fell quiet for a moment, his face lined with pain. "Maybe she wasn't as impressed with me as I thought. Maybe she had someone else waiting in the wings."

"And that's why you strangled her?"

His thoughts still of Letty, Joe did not rise to Vickers's bait but shook his head. "No. She was fine when I left on Thursday."

After allowing a few moments of silence, Vickers tossed his pen on the table and leaned back in his seat, his arm draped casually over the high, chair back. "Have sex with her?"

The question only ignited Joe's anger again. "You mind your own bloody business, Vickers. Concentrate on who might have strangled her, not my private life…" Awareness slipped through his mind. His anger faded and a broad, cynical smile spread across his crinkled features. "Oh, I get it now. This is a Sanford Valentine Strangler crime, isn't it?" A blush came to Vickers's face, and Joe became more serious, his eyes burning in to them. "This nutter has struck again, hasn't he? How many is it now? Three? Four? One a year for the last how many years? And you think it's me?" He laughed harshly, but there was no humour in the bark. "I knew you were desperate for suspects, Vickers, but I didn't know you were that hard up. According to the papers, the guy rapes them before he kills them. That means you have tons of DNA. Go ahead and check mine against it all. You'll find it doesn't match."

"The newspapers don't always get it right," Vickers countered. "You're right, of course. The murder of Mrs Hill has all the hallmarks of the Sanford Valentine Strangler, but they're not difficult to mimic. But, as always, we withhold certain facts from the media; facts which only the guilty person would know." He leaned forward and jabbed a large index finger into the table top. "A lack of body fluids doesn't prove your innocence, Murray."

Joe puzzled over the admission for a moment before the answer occurred to him. "So he doesn't have sex with them before he kills them. Either that or he uses a condom." He was speaking as much to himself as the two officers. "In that case, you still find traces of the lubricant in her, er… Well, you know what I mean. That means these are not sex killings, unless he's getting off in some strange way with it." His eyes homed in on Vickers. "Is that it?"

"We were hoping you could tell us."

"Gar." Joe waved a dismissive hand at the chief inspector. "Don't talk so bloody soft, man. You know it isn't me. And as far as I'm concerned, if you've no more questions to ask, then I'm going. Someone has to find out who killed these women."

Vickers snapped off the recorders. "You will mind your own business."

Feeling himself with a measure of control, Joe smiled and shook his head. "You're joking, aren't you? You drag me away from my livelihood, ask me these idiot questions, most of 'em designed to trap me into some kind of admission, and then, when you admit defeat, you tell me to keep out of it. You should try running a workman's café for a month or two, Vickers. It won't help your investigative skills, but at least you'd get a taste of real life."

***

With Joe gone, Vickers grumbled, "One of these days…"

Gemma rounded on him. "Sir, with all due respect, you do not come to Sanford and hassle a man like Joe Murray the way you just did."

"Be careful, Sergeant."

"No, sir, I will not be careful. And if I have to, I'll go to the

Chief Superintendent with this. I may only be a sergeant, but I am the senior CID officer in Sanford, and I know these people. You tackle a man like Joe, and they will rally round him. He's cranky, ill-tempered, outspoken and tight-fisted, but he's not universally disliked. Just the opposite, in fact. We need the public's co-operation in this investigation, and we both know my Uncle Joe wouldn't hurt a fly, let alone murder middle-aged women."

Vickers glowered at her. "You shouldn't even be involved in this investigation, Craddock. Unfortunately, as you've just pointed out, you're the senior officer on the ground in Sanford, and we need your local knowledge. But just remember your duty. It comes before family and friends. Joe Murray is a suspect. He was one of the last people to see Letty Hill alive, and he's just admitted he spent the night with her. He is a suspect and he remains one until I say otherwise."

Gemma struggled to rein in her temper. "He'll start shoving his nose in. If only to clear his name. It's not always good news when Joe investigates. There are times when he does more harm than good, but equally, there are those times when he comes up with vital information. You should know. He did it to you in Wakefield, the year before last. Now, thanks to your heavy boots, whatever he learns, he'll keep to himself."

"This is your last warning, Sergeant. If you're so sure of his innocence, then get out there and prove it."

Gemma gathered together her belongings. "Thank you, sir. I'll do just that."

Chapter Four

The Lazy Luncheonette was in the deepest throes of the lunchtime rush when Joe got back.

Changing quickly into his whites, he relieved Sheila at the counter, freeing her to deliver the orders, and as they coped with the queues, he tried, as best he could, to bring his companions up to date, but it was after two, with the last of the day's meal served, and custom quietening down, before he could properly tell them the full tale.

They hung on his every word. Even Lee, who finished at two and normally went straight home, stayed behind to listen.

When he had told them everything, Joe looked fondly on his nephew. "You're a good lad, Lee, and I need you to do me a favour, if you will. I need you to bring Cheryl in, if she's not busy with anything else, to cover for the next few days."

"You're not going to prison are you, Uncle Joe?"

Joe's fondness almost evaporated in the face of his nephew's dim-wittedness. "No, boy, I am not going to prison, but Chief Inspector Vickers will try his damndest to make sure I do. But to stay out of prison means I'm gonna have to devote a lot of time to investigating this business, and that means I'll be AWOL for much of the coming week. If Cheryl could cover, I'd be grateful."

"Shouldn't be a problem," Lee said with a broad smile. "She'll get her mum to look after Danny. I'll see you all tomorrow."

With Lee gone, Joe, Sheila and Brenda mulled over the worrying events.

"That poor woman," Brenda said. "The fourth now. It's time they found this pervert and locked him away."

Joe hedged his words. "Listen, Brenda, don't take this the wrong way, but you should be careful. You're, er, slightly freer with your... favours, let's say, than Sheila and me. Just be careful who you're dating."

Brenda smiled weakly. "I'm not worried, Joe. He only kills on Valentine's Night, so I'm safe for another year."

"We don't know that for sure," Joe said. "Even Vickers admits it's odd for a serial killer to go a whole year at a time without another victim."

"And talking of Vickers, he doesn't seriously suspect you, does he?" Sheila asked as she and Brenda got up and began work on cleaning down.

Joe shook his head and gulped down a mouthful of tea as the next customer walked in. Serving the woman with a cup of tea and a slice of Lee's homemade apple pie, Joe replied to Sheila.

"No, I don't think he does. I think he's still annoyed at the Wakefield jewellery affair when I told him a few home truths, then pinned the culprit down before him."

"I thought you came out of that, sort of, friendly," Brenda said.

Joe dropped the customer's five-pound note in the till, and gave her change. "There you go, luv. Enjoy." Replying, to Brenda, he went on, "Vickers thanked me for my help, but it was grudging. In fact, he described it more as interference. It would give him great pleasure to see me charged with something."

The local news appeared on the wall-mounted, flat screen TV. Sheila reached for the remote and turned up the volume.

"Police in Sanford have questioned a man on the death of fifty-three-year-old Letitia Hill. Joseph Murray, a businessman, was questioned at Sanford Police station this morning. Chief Inspector Roy Vickers of West Yorkshire CID said no charges were brought,

and Mr Murray was later released pending further inquiries. Mrs Hill, a widow, is believed to be the fourth victim of the Sanford Valentine Strangler."

While the newscaster moved onto other local stories, Sheila turned the volume down again. The woman customer, who had watched the report, stood and left, her pie and tea untouched. Behind the counter, his face vermillion with rage, Joe snatched up his mobile and called the police station.

"It's Joe Murray. Put me through to Vickers," he barked.

"I'm sorry, Mr Murray, but I don't know if he'll—"

"Tell him if he doesn't speak to me now, I'll go to the press and tell them exactly who made him look a fool in Wakefield the year before last."

"Hold on a minute, sir."

Waiting to be connected, Joe paced furiously behind the counter. Two workmen entered. Brenda, responding to years of automatism, left her cleaning and joined Joe to serve them, while Joe ducked into the kitchen, still bubbling angrily.

"Chief Inspector Vickers."

"Vickers, it's Joe Murray. What the hell are you playing at bandying my name all over the TV?"

"I was reporting to the press, Murray. It's standard procedure."

"It's already costing me business," Joe shouted. "And you didn't have to name me."

"Joe in a spot of bother is he, Brenda?" one of the workmen asked.

She shushed him as she passed over his beaker of tea. "You know Joe. He'll sort it."

On the telephone, Vickers remained calm in the face of Joe's onslaught. "No one has accused you of anything, Murray. We've simply given out a statement saying you've been questioned. If your customers don't like being served by a suspect in a murder inquiry, that's not my fault."

"We'll see what my lawyers have to say about that when I

work out the damage you're doing. You know damn well it isn't me. You had no business naming me."

"Tell it to the Chief Constable."

"I will. Freddie Wainman happens to be an old friend."

"I mean the Chief Constable of West Yorkshire, not the Assistant Chief Constable of North Yorkshire."

"They all pee in the same pot," Joe retorted, "and by the time I've done, the pot they're aiming at will be on your head."

"Just calm down," Vickers advised. "I'm sending your niece to see you."

"And getting Gemma to shut me up won't work."

"I'm not trying to shut you up," Vickers replied. "You'll see why I've sent her when she gets there."

"She'd better be carrying a large cheque," Joe snapped, and cut the call off.

As he came back into the café, where Brenda and Sheila were once more engaged in the cleaning down, one of the two workmen grinned at him. "What's up, Joe? Do they think you're the Valentine Strangler?"

"I've been questioned on it," Joe grumbled.

The other workman gaped. "You're joking."

"No I'm not bloody joking. Are you gonna walk out, too?"

The first workman smiled again and held his beaker forward. "No, but would you mind tasting my tea… just to be sure."

From across the café, Brenda laughed. "Idiot. The Valentine Strangler strangles his victims. He doesn't poison them."

"Sod off all of you," Joe snapped and stormed out into the street where he could enjoy a cigarette.

The day was fresh, but bitterly cold, in direct contrast to Joe's boiling mood. A stiff, easterly wind drove broken cloud across a volatile sky, occasional patches of sunshine showing through, fighting against the icy chill.

Barely noticing the wind, he paced back and forth across the front of his premises, puffing irritably on his hand-rolled cigarette, muttering incoherently to himself at the perceived injustice of the morning's events, occasionally pausing to reflect on the wonderful night he had enjoyed with Letty, and the terrible swiftness with which her life had been taken. And if his thoughts, as bitter as the east wind whipping the buildings of Britannia Parade, were of the solitary life he faced after such a short relationship, it did not take long for them to settle on Letty, and the sorrow for her life lost.

"Fifty-three is no age to die," he grumbled.

Crushing out his cigarette, he went back into the café as the two workmen left, still pulling his leg, and pitched in to help Sheila and Brenda with the daily cleaning. Muttering mutinously to himself, his anger gave added power to his scrubbing. Not trusting himself to remain civil, he left the few customers who came in to his companions.

By three thirty, with the cleaning done, they were back at table five, enjoying a last cup of tea, when Gemma entered carrying her briefcase.

Brenda poured Gemma a cup of tea. "Thank God you're here. He's been like a bear with a sore doodah ever since he came back from the police station this morning."

"That bloody Vickers," Joe growled. "Naming me like that."

"Calm down, Uncle Joe. Mr Vickers did not do anything against the law or the rules. We're investigating a murder, you were one of the last people to see Mrs Hill alive, and there are traces of you all over her house. We had to speak to you."

"You didn't have to broadcast it, though, did you?" Joe protested. "Vickers did it on purpose."

Gemma sighed. "Nobody accused you of anything, Uncle Joe."

"I'm losing custom," he cried.

"One person walked out," Sheila said.

"Really?"

"Yes," Brenda said. "But she'd paid for her tea and cake and she didn't ask for her money back."

"And the cake went back in the chiller," Sheila told Gemma.

Joe glowered "I did not put that apple pie back in the cold cupboard."

"I know you didn't," Sheila replied. "Brenda did."

Joe glanced sharply at Brenda.

"She hadn't touched it," Brenda argued, "and I wasn't about to see good food go to waste."

Joe shook his head. "Between you and Vickers, you'll put me out of business." He stood up. "I'm going for another smoke."

"No, stay there, Uncle Joe," Gemma insisted. "And please calm down. You'll have a heart attack the way you're going on."

"That would bugger up Vickers, wouldn't it? He'd have to look for a proper suspect then."

Gemma reached into her briefcase and from it took a buff folder. "For your information, Chief Inspector Vickers sent me to you. I don't know whether he's just winding you up with this TV business, but he's not a complete fool. He knows how observant you are, and we need your powers of observation."

"So I can sell myself down the river? Go back to Gale Street, Gemma, and tell Vickers to shove it."

"Just shut up and listen," Gemma said, venting her frustration through gritted teeth. Pausing a moment to calm down, she went on, "We know you were at Letty's all night on Wednesday. You told us so."

Brenda grinned. "Caught out again, Joe. Don't you know you'll never be able to hide from me?"

"Please, Mrs Jump. I'm gonna be here all night at this rate." Switching her attention back to Joe, Gemma explained, "Like I said, we've found traces of you all over the house, including the bedroom, bathroom and living room. We can't let you back in there, but Vickers has asked me to show you photographs from the place so that you can tell us if there's anything that doesn't tally with your memory." A look of caution entered her eyes. "You may find some of these pictures, er, disturbing."

"I've seen bodies before," Joe retorted. "Real ones, not just photographs. Come on. Show me."

He was wrong. The first photograph sent a shockwave of distress through him. It was an image of Letty laid flat on her back, her skirt pushed up, empty eyes staring at the ceiling, black cord wrapped around her neck. Joe bit his lip and look away, grimacing his anger and grief.

"I'm sorry, Uncle Joe," Gemma said. "I must ask you to look at the photograph. Tell me if there is anything not right."

"For God's sake…"

"Please."

Joe forced himself to look again.

"He doesn't know the colour of her knickers, I can tell you that," Brenda joked, oblivious to Joe's pain.

His anger boiled over again. "When I got into bed with her, she wasn't wearing any." He put the photograph down and pushed it to Brenda, turning it so she could see it the right way up.

Brenda stared. The colour drained from her cheeks, and any humour she had felt left her shocked face. "Oh, dear God." Tears sparkled in her eye. "I'm… I'm sorry, Joe. I never realised… oh dear." She reached into the pocket of her tabard, seeking a tissue.

Made of slightly sterner stuff, Sheila, too, looked at the large image, her features set in stone. She patted Brenda's arm.

"Anything, Uncle Joe?"

"I don't know," he sighed. "I just wasn't taking much notice. You know. You don't, do you? We'd had a few beers, she invited me in for a nightcap, one thing led to another, and… well you know. All I can tell you, Gemma, is what I told you at the station. She was fine when I left her yesterday morning."

Gemma fished into her folder again, and drew out several large prints of the living room, bedroom, and one of the kitchen showing the stainless steel sink, a cup and saucer racked up on the drainer. "Take a look at these. See if anything comes to mind."

Joe glanced, looked closer, then shook his head. "I don't have a photographic memory, Gemma. Sure we were in the living room for a while before… And I used the bathroom, and the kitchen, but I just wasn't taking much notice of anything. What about the ligature?"

"Hmm, curious," Gemma admitted. "It's a length of cord. We think it comes from a retractable dog leash. You know the kind of thing. They're usually five metres long, and the cord extends as the dog moves away, then rewinds into the handle when it comes back to you. This is a heavy duty one, usually used for large dogs. The killer cut about a metre of the cord off, but here's an oddity. It's been washed."

Sheila's eyebrows rose. "Washed?"

"Yes. It's as if someone has rubbed it down with a damp cloth coated in washing up liquid. No extraneous marks, finger marks or palm marks on it at all."

Now Joe was surprised. "I shouldn't have thought you'd get prints off a thing that narrow."

"You'd be surprised what we can get off something like that," Gemma reported. "On this kind of thing, we'd expect a few dog hairs. That might have given us a tiny lead on the breed of dog. But…" she shrugged. "Nothing."

"He was obviously wearing gloves, then," Brenda commented, tucking the tissue back in her coverall.

"All the time, Mrs Jump," Gemma agreed. "We know nothing, we have nothing. Mrs Hill is the fourth victim of this man, assuming it is the same man, and we're fairly certain of that."

"You're certain it's not a copycat?" Joe asked.

Gemma shook her head. "Remember Vickers told you we keep certain information from the press? The way he leaves his victims, skirts up, knickers, stockings showing, is something we don't tell them. The fact that he never, *never* leaves any sign of sexual activity, is something else."

The light dawned in Joe's eyes. "That's what Vickers meant when he said a lack of bodily emissions would prove nothing."

"Correct. The idea that the victims were raped and murdered is an invention of the media. No one from our department has ever said anything of the kind, and I'd appreciate it if you three would keep it to yourselves."

"So they're not, er, sex killings?" Sheila's ears coloured at the mere suggestion.

"The truth is, Mrs Riley, we don't know. It could be that the killer gets off, for want of a better phrase, after murdering them and pushing up their skirts. If so, he leaves no trace."

"He must leave some evidence of himself," Joe protested.

"Tons of it we imagine," Gemma said. "But these are ordinary women in ordinary houses, Uncle Joe. For instance, Mrs Riley, you're a widow. How many men do you have in your house in the space of, say, a month?"

Sheila entire face coloured this time. "I don't have any men, Gemma. And I object—"

"No, no. You're misunderstanding me. I said men, not men friends or lovers. TV repairmen, washing machine engineers, plumbers, central heating repairs, and so on. Callers collecting for charity, insurance salespeople. Anyone like that."

"Oh. I see what you mean." Sheila calmed a little. "I suppose, quite a few."

"You see, Uncle Joe. We have to piece together the last few weeks of the victims' lives and they all lived alone, so it's not easy. And over the last three years, we've worked to identify those tiny clues which may have come from the same person."

"Without success?" Joe asked.

"Nothing we could get DNA or a blood type from,"

Gemma admitted. "Threads which may have come from a coat or jumper. Shoe impressions on the carpets which only show up under ultra-violet." Gemma chewed her lip. "Thelma Warburton had been dead four days when we got to her. We got next to nothing from her or her house. This man is ultra-careful. I'm surprised he doesn't vacuum the house after he's done."

"Never any sign of a struggle?" Joe wanted to know.

Gemma shook her head. "Not even the death struggle."

"Then, obviously, the women knew him. Even Letty."

"Correct, but we've drawn a complete blank there, too. We cannot find one person common to all four women, and although we haven't really begun checking Letty's background, we're certain the four women did not know each other."

Allowing his thoughts to run, Joe fiddled with a photograph of the mock fireplace in Letty's living room. "Whatever you're looking for, the link, is so tiny it's all but insignificant, then. You're sure he doesn't just choose his victims at random?"

"Very unlikely," Gemma replied. "Middle-aged, single women, living alone, no known relationships? No, Uncle Joe, he has to know something about them in advance."

Joe had stopped listening. He was concentrating on the photograph. In the centre of the mantelpiece stood the small clock with its dark, mahogany-coloured surround. From one side of it projected what looked like a piece of white card.

"What's that?" He turned the photograph and pointed so Gemma could see what he was asking about.

"Not sure," she said, and dipped into her briefcase again, coming out with a printed list. "This is a list of everything in the house. Let's see..." She ran her finger down the list. "Not the Valentine Card. We know about that... Could be her dentist's appointment card... No. Here it is. It's a business card. SDA. The Sanford Dating Agency."

Joe's frown returned. "She was using a dating agency?"

"Well, we don't know for sure. Not yet. It's a line of inquiry. That's not how you met her?"

"No. I told you, she was a new member of the 3rd Age Club."

"Maybe she was a member of the dating agency before she joined your club."

"Yeah, and maybe she was just taking the mick with me on Wednesday night."

Brenda, her face serious this time, said, "There's nothing wrong with one-night stands, Joe. You're the odd man out expecting something more just because she jumped into bed with you."

Gemma gathered together the photographs and put them back in her briefcase. Snapping the locks shut, she stood up. "If you think of anything, Uncle Joe, please get in touch with us. I'm sure Vickers will eliminate you from the inquiries quickly. I'll leave you to it…. Oh. One other thing. Please, please don't go poking your nose in. This man is dangerous."

Joe snorted. "Dangerous? I'll give him dangerous when I get my hands on him."

With a wry shake of the head, Gemma walked out. Joe got to his feet, gathered the cups together and moved them to the kitchen.

"Dangerous, my eye," Brenda smiled. "Joe, even as a kid you couldn't punch your way out of a paper bag."

"No, but my gang was the toughest in the school. I'll get George and Owen to back me up."

Sheila wagged a disapproving finger at him. "Listen to your niece, Joe. She's talking common sense."

"And you're talking as daft as Vickers. Do you seriously expect me to mind my own business after I've been publicly accused of murder. Not likely." Joe ran water into the sink. "Lock up, will you Sheila. Then you two can get off if you want. I'll finish these odd few pots."

Sheila moved to the door, but before she could lock it, Les

Tanner walked in.

"Hello, Les," she greeted.

"We're shut," Joe called from the kitchen.

"Quite all right, Murray," Les replied. "I don't want anything. I came here to deliver some news."

Drying his hands on a tea towel, Joe came out of the kitchen. "What? What is it?"

Les usually took great delight in goading Joe, and the two had been at loggerheads for as long as anyone could recall, usually over Joe's running of the Sanford 3rd Age Club. This time, however, the former Territorial Army Captain appeared reluctant and diffident.

"I, er, I caught the news bulletins earlier in the day."

"Yes, well, don't believe everything you hear, Les."

"No. Of course not. I'm not the only one, Murray. A couple of members rang me at the town hall, after which I rang a few others, and the consensus is they want an extraordinary meeting, eight o'clock this evening, at the Miner's Arms."

Brenda had already second-guessed what was coming and her features darkened. "Why?"

"I, er, I'm sorry, Joe." That signalled bad news to Joe. Tanner never called him by his first name. "I'll repeat verbatim what was said to me. The Sanford 3rd Age Club does not want a murder suspect as its Chair."

Chapter Five

Joe glared at Tanner. "This is your doing. You've been trying to get me out for years."

Sitting opposite Joe, Tanner held up both hands in a gesture of innocence. "No. No. You're wrong. It's true I don't think you're a particularly good Chairperson. I've never made any secret of my opinion, and I believe I could do better, but I did not instigate this issue. I merely followed up one or two complaints to judge the feeling of the membership."

"Who made the original complaint, Les?" Sheila asked.

"Morton Norris. He rang me shortly after he'd seen the news."

Joe scowled. "How the hell did Mort see the news? He works on the market."

"He was in the bar of the Flagstaff Inn apparently," Tanner said. "I don't see what difference that makes. If he hadn't seen it there, he would have caught it when he got home and he would still have rung me. Ten minutes later, Stewart Dalmer rang, saying Morton had spoken to him and he felt the same way. Not long after that, Irene Pyecock called and told me she and Norman were worried about you running the club while you were under suspicion of murder. From there, I rang Mavis Barker and Cyril Peck, and they were in broad agreement. Sylvia refuses to believe that you're guilty and, naturally, I share that opinion. I know you're no murderer. On the other hand, I could tell from Sylvia's tone of voice that she has her reservations on the issue of you carrying on while this business is hanging over you."

"This suits you, though, Les," Brenda insisted.

Tanner would not hear it. "Brenda, if ever I'm to take over the running of the club, I'd rather do so on merit. Joe has his supporters. Owen Frickley wasn't prepared to commit himself, and George Robson told me to… Well, you know George. Alec Staines will be there, and he's in your corner. What I'm saying, and I admit it was my idea, is let's get an extraordinary meeting together tonight, and decide the matter properly."

Joe pulled himself together. "All right. We'll ring as many of the members as we can."

Sheila chewed her lip. "I'd better dig out the articles. To make any changes, we need a quorum in attendance."

"What's the quorum?" Joe asked.

"The minimum number of members required to commit binding changes," Tanner explained.

Joe fumed. "I know what *a* quorum is. I'm asking what *the* quorum is for the Sanford 3rd Age Club."

"Fifty… I think. Like I said, I'll check on it," Sheila replied. She concentrated on the captain. "Les, we're old friends. All of us. For that reason I think you should know in advance of the way I will vote. I'm firmly on Joe's side. He's been a good chairman, and I feel it's thoroughly reprehensible of the members to come down on him because of this silly news story."

"Hear, hear," Brenda said, slipping prematurely into the formal language of the committee meeting.

Tanner smiled. "Curiously enough, I agree with you, and you have my assurance, I will not stand against you. But the club is not run for any particular individual. It's a collective and the will of the membership is what counts." He got to his feet again. "The Miner's Arms at eight o'clock, then."

With a stiff, military nod to all of them, Tanner turned and marched out.

The two women sat with Joe. Brenda took his hand this time. "We're with you, Joe."

He nodded vaguely, vacantly. "Keep telling me how much fun we have running the 3rd Age Club. I keep forgetting."

"Tonight will not be fun," Sheila declared. "Tonight will be all out war, and certain people are going to get a piece of my mind." She stood up. "If you'll both excuse me, I'll get off home. I need to check those articles and I need to canvas some support."

She passed through to the kitchen, hung up her tabard, and put on her coat. Coming back into the café, she looked pointedly at Brenda, who shook her head. "I'll give it a minute or two."

Joe let Sheila out and locked the door behind her. With the time turned four thirty, the chilly day was settling in what promised to be another bitterly cold night. He gazed out on the increasing traffic of the Friday rush, their lights cutting through the gathering dusk, and fervently wished, for once, that he were a part of it. Those motorists would go home with routine problems on their minds: wives, girlfriends, children, mortgages. They didn't have to face dealing with the accounts, dealing with a potential murder charge, dealing with a mob of unruly, born again, middle-aged teenagers.

He rejoined Brenda, and she took his hand again. "What are we gonna do with you, Joe?"

"Buy me a one-way ticket to Brazil?"

She smiled wanly. "Never lose it, Joe. That sense of humour. You may be a cynic, but it's what makes you special. Listen, I was thinking, there's no way you're just going to let these killings pass is there?"

"Vickers told me to mind my own business, and you can guess what I said to him. You heard me say it to Gemma, earlier."

"Precisely. But this is my specialist area, Joe." Releasing his hand, she pressed hers to her heart. "I know a lot of people just think I'm a randy widow, but it's not true… well, not entirely true. I like dating, I know about dating. I was thinking I could—"

"Set yourself up as a possible target?"

Brenda blushed. "Well, something like that."

Joe shook his head and smiled. "You'd have a hell of a long wait. He only strikes over Valentine... according to Vickers. And even if he's busier than we think, do you seriously imagine I'd let you put yourself in danger?" He tapped his temple with a bony finger. "Get real, Brenda, and get smart. There is no way I would put either of you at risk." He laughed. "Besides, if the Valentine Strangler bumped you off, who would I get to help Lee in the kitchen?"

Brenda laughed too. "The offer is there, Joe."

"Thanks, but no thanks." He got to his feet. "You get off home. I have to cash up and do the books before the Miner's Arms."

Brenda moved to the kitchen and took off her tabard. "All right," she said, putting on her coat. "If I can't help you with the killings, at least let me rip into those ungrateful buggers." Digging through her pockets, she returned to Joe and tossed a large bundle of keys on the table. "Don't want to take your keys home with me, Joe. People will talk."

"You should have a spare set anyway."

"For the Lazy Luncheonette, yes, but for your apartment? I don't think so."

Picking up the keys, Joe grunted again. "You have a key to Sheila's place in case she takes ill. What happens if I'm ill?"

"You've got Lee and Cheryl, and a reputation that's bad enough already. I'll see you tonight, Joe."

***

By eight forty-five, the air in the top room of the Miner's Arms was thick with argument, counterargument, frayed tempers, and intimidation from both sides. George Robson, a burly gardener employed by the borough, had twice been warned for threatening Morton Norris with physical violence, and Mort had twice been told to put his coat back on after taking it off and daring George to, "Come and try your luck, tubby."

The landlord, Mick Chadwick, was run off his feet keeping the members topped up in drink, Sheila and Brenda struggled to maintain order so that the different speakers could be heard, and Joe was ready to throw the towel in.

Soon after the doors were closed, Sheila ran a head count via tellers Les Tanner and Cyril Peck, and confirmed that there were seventy-eight members in attendance.

"The quorum is fifty, Joe," she told him, "so whatever decisions are reached tonight, they will be binding. And under the terms of the articles, a simple majority will suffice. If more than thirty-nine vote you out, you're out."

It rapidly became clear that a hard core of about twenty-five members wanted Joe to stand down, while a similar number were firm in their support."

"That leaves somewhere around thirty don't knows," Brenda said while they were listening to Morton Norris's demands for Joe's resignation. "It could go either way."

When Morton had finished, Brenda stood in Joe's defence.

"This man has worked tirelessly for you ever since the club was first founded. He negotiates all your outings, and he's secured some big discounts. He liaises with the hotels and the bus company, helps sort out your itineraries, he secures theatre tickets, again at nice prices, and as if that isn't enough, he haggles with our landlord –" She waved an arm in the direction of Mick Chadwick "– for the hire of this room to put on your weekly disco, which he also hosts. And he's never taken so much as a free drink for any of his work. Now he has a problem, and you want to throw him out?"

"Nobody suggests he should resign from the club," Mort Norris called out. "Just the Chair."

Mort's declaration met with murmurs of approval, quickly

joined by louder mumbles of disagreement.

"He hasn't done anything wrong," Brenda pointed out.

"He's been arrested on suspicion of murder," Stewart Dalmer responded quickly. "That could reflect badly on the club. Remember, the news bulletins travel a lot further than just Sanford."

"We're a club," Joe protested. "It's not like we have a share price to worry about. And we're restricted to the Sanford area."

"I'm not thinking of membership drives," Dalmer retorted. "I'm thinking of hotels and other venues. Brenda has just said that you do most of the negotiating, Joe. The moment these places hear your name, they could turn us away."

"I've been questioned, not charged."

"It's all over the media," Mort reiterated.

His gorge rising, Joe demanded, "Have you been questioned yet?"

Mort appeared puzzled. "No. I didn't know her."

"Yes you did. You all knew her…"

Sheila leaned into him and whispered, "This is a bad approach, Joe."

He ignored her and addressed the members again. "A good many of you were with us on Wednesday evening at Churchill's."

"We didn't sleep with her," Dalmer pointed out, and Joe blushed.

"Told you," Sheila muttered.

Dalmer continued to press home his side's advantage. "A number of us would prefer to see someone like Captain Tanner in the Chair. It's as simple as that."

"And a fair few of us wouldn't," George Robson barked. "Most of us wanna see Joe stay where he is."

"To drag the club down into the gutter?" Dalmer demanded.

"No, to stop toffee-nosed twonks like you taking it over," George retorted, and tempers began to rise again.

Brenda called them to order and Les Tanner took the floor.

"Mr Dalmer, ladies and gentlemen, if you'd hear me out, please." He waited for the rhubarb rumblings to subside. "I've challenged Joe Murray for the Chair in the past, and it's common knowledge that I don't like his lack of organisation. I believe I could do better. However, I am not prepared to stand in opposition to him on this matter. I think you have a point, Mr Dalmer, on the way in which this business will reflect on STAC, but I refuse to be recognised as the man who could only secure the Chair by taking advantage of unfortunate circumstances surrounding the present incumbent. If I am to beat Joe Murray and take over the running of this club, then it will be on merit."

"Very well, then," Dalmer replied when a fresh hubbub had settled. "I'll ask other members to propose me as Chair."

"Proposed," Mort Norris said.

Tanner ignored Mort and spoke directly to Dalmer. "Do you have the relevant experience?"

"I was head of English at Sanford College of Further Education for twenty years. I think I know something about organisation and administration."

Another chorus of angry exchanges broke out. Sheila, Brenda and Tanner concentrated on Joe.

"We're faced with a coup d'état," Sheila pointed out in a whisper, "and we have to stop it."

"If you have any ides, I'm listening," Tanner said, and the other two agreed.

"As a matter of fact, I have," Sheila told them.

They went into a huddle while Sheila expounded her idea. Throughout the room, the rumblings continued, even at the bar where many members fled to replenish their drinks.

At length Sheila stood before the members and called them to order again.

"We propose a compromise solution, which we hope you will all find acceptable. First, we suggest that Joe be granted leave of absence from his position as Chair, in order to let him sort out his problems and clear his name. Second, we propose that Captain Tanner stand in for Joe, *pro tem*. Finally, we propose a review of the situation in one month."

Dalmer stood again. "And suppose Mr Murray hasn't been able to sort out his problems by then?"

Joe took front and centre. "In that case, I will resign and we'll hold a leadership election."

The announcement was greeted with murmurs of approval from the floor.

"Can we hold a vote on the proposal, ladies and gentlemen. Tellers, please."

Tanner and Cyril Peck situated themselves on either side of the room.

"Those in favour?"

Hands shot up around the room. There was a delay while Tanner and Cyril counted them, and compared their results. Tanner made a note of the figure and nodded to Sheila.

"Those against?"

Hand rose again but even from the podium, Joe could see they were fewer in number than the last vote.

Tanner and Cyril consulted once again. Tanner made a note of the figure and then approached the podium. Turning to face the members, he declared, "Those in favour, sixty-one, those against, seventeen. The motion to allow Joe Murray leave of absence, is carried by a majority of forty-four."

A loud cheer erupted from Joe's hardcore supporters, and the room subsided into busy chatter.

"Thanks, Les," Joe said stepping from the dais.

"Ah, you may not be so thankful the next time you come up for re-election, Joe. The gloves will be off then."

"Well, at least we got it all sorted," Brenda chirped. "All you have to do, Joe, is clear your name and we can go back to normal."

Joe gazed out across the crowd of members, many of them

still arguing. "Or as normal as this lot could ever get."

***

A part of Joe's success in the Chair of the Sanford 3rd Age Club, was his ingrained knowledge of his members. He knew most of them personally, and as a collective he understood them. It was that knowledge which had prompted him to bring his disco computer along to the meeting. An ordinary laptop, it had programs other than basic software; sound system, karaoke software and thousands and thousands of songs, mostly from the fifties, sixties and seventies.

Wednesday night was the official weekly disco, except when outings such as Churchill's were scheduled for Wednesday. They had missed their disco this week, and in bringing the laptop, Joe had known that once the extraordinary meeting was over and the doors opened, his members would be looking for some music and dance to go with their drink.

Mick Chadwick, the landlord, had already been paid for the use of the room and readily agreed to the impromptu disco. "Anything to sell more ale."

Within five minutes, the music of Danny Williams singing *Moon River* blared from the speakers, and Joe marvelled at the sudden party atmosphere of the members.

"A quarter of an hour ago, they were tearing each other to pieces. Now look at 'em. Best of friends."

"I always believe that's the hallmark of true friendship," Sheila said. "When you can disagree and still remain friends."

"Nah," Joe disagreed. "The mark of a true friend is one who doesn't ask you to dip into your wallet when he's broke."

Brenda tutted at the ceiling. "Didn't take you long to get back on form, either, did it?" she swallowed a generous helping of Campari and soda. "So come on, Sherlock, we've solved one of your problems tonight, how are we going to find the slimeball who killed Letty and those other poor women?"

"Slimeball?" Sheila's eyebrows shot up. "You've been watching American films again, haven't you?"

Brenda smacked her lips. "Oh yes. I'll tell you what, that Mel Gibson could—"

"Let's stick to the Valentine Strangler, eh?" Joe interrupted. "This is a different matter to the kinda thing we normally deal with. We're not in a hotel, we're at home, it's been going on for four years and there are no suspects… Correction, there are thousands of suspects. Almost every man in Sanford."

"With the exception of you."

"With the exception of me." Joe rolled a cigarette. "The chances of us finding him are remote."

"So you're just going to let it go?" Brenda asked.

"When have you ever known me to do that? Of course I'm not going to let it go. Not while Vickers has me marked down as prime suspect. I'm just saying it'll not be as easy as other cases we've cracked, and much of the trail will be cold. Even that leading from Letty's place. To evade the plod this long, the guy must be ultra-careful. You think about all the other cases we've handled. Amateurs, the lot of 'em. This guy is a pro. He must be or the cops would have something on him by now." He tucked the cigarette in his shirt pocket and reached for his topcoat. "And why else would Vickers be in a hurry to pin it on me?"

Brenda considered this for a moment. "Because he doesn't like you."

Sheila tittered. "There is that, but to be fair, Brenda, the police don't usually let their personal feelings clutter up an investigation."

"I'll think about it while I'm having a smoke," Joe promised and put his coat on. "Back in ten minutes."

Leaving the room, Joe made his way downstairs and out through the lounge bar to the smoke shelter on the car park, where he found Stewart Dalmer puffing contentedly on his pipe.

"It was nothing personal up there, Joe." Dalmer greeted him.

Joe joined him at a wooden table under the single, overhead heater, which glowed a dull red against the black backdrop of the chilly night. "No. Course not, Stewart."

"I had the best interests of the club at heart."

Joe lit his cigarette. "You're happy with the compromise?"

Dalmer nodded and took the pipe from between his lips. "It's what we English are best at," he said with a broad smile. "Compromise."

"Take one Englishman and you have an idiot. Two Englishmen, you have a committee."

Dalmer laughed. "Three Englishmen and you have an empire. It's an old quote, attributed to Hermann Göring, but I believe he said two Englishmen formed a club, not a committee."

Joe shrugged. "Same difference." He drew on his cigarette and blew out a thin cloud of smoke. "You knew Letty Hill, didn't you?"

Dalmer examined the bowl of his pipe, put it back into his mouth and lit it. When it was satisfactorily smoking again, he put his lighter away. "I had a few dinner dates with her, that's all. Nothing serious. And that's… oh… over a year ago, now."

"How did you meet her?" Joe asked. "Was it through the Sanford Dating Agency?"

Dalmer laughed again. "Good heavens, no. I met her at the college."

"College?" Joe puffed on his cigarette."I didn't know she was a teacher. She told me—"

"She enrolled in an adult leisure class, Joe," Dalmer interrupted. "Literary appreciation. We were reading Thackeray's *Vanity Fair* that term… er, have you read it?"

Joe shook his head."No. sorry. Conan Doyle, Agatha Christie, even Mickey Spillane, but not Thackeray."

"Pulp fiction," Dalmer muttered with a sight air of disdain.

"Not the kind of literature we discuss at the Artesian Well."

"The where?"

"My favourite pub. It's in Wakefield." Dalmer gestured at the building around them. "Much better class of patron than this place. More educated; all of them. Anyway, back to Letty and the leisure classes. The idea of the class was we all read the same book across a period of one term, and each week we would meet to discuss it; the way it reflects society at the time of writing, what set it apart from other, similar novels. You know the kind of thing. It was a different book each term. We'd done Steinbeck's *Grapes of Wrath* the term before, but Letty wasn't with us, then. She preferred English novels to American, and she was particularly enthusiastic about *Vanity Fair*."

"You make it sound as if most of the class weren't."

Dalmer nodded slowly. "That is so, and you can include me amongst that number. Thackeray was never one of my favourites, but the Local Education Authority set the reading, not me."

Joe was surprised once again. "What? Even for a leisure class?"

"Even for a leisure class. There was a good deal of, shall we say, snobbery about the members of the committee. I always felt we could have encouraged more people by reading *A Clockwork Orange*, but…" He trailed off and shrugged.

"So you met Letty there."

"Hmm, yes. I invited her out for dinner, she accepted. I think we met two or three times, but it was obvious, at least to me, that the woman was more interested in Thackeray than me, so I allowed things to die their natural death. We remained fairly good friends, of course, but it was never more than that."

"Interesting. She told me you made her an offer for some antique spoons."

Dalmer nodded. "I buy and sell antiques. A hobby more

than anything." He grinned. "No sale. Those spoons had a sentimental value far greater than their cash equivalent."

"She told me so." Joe's cigarette had gone out. Relighting it, he fiddled with his brass Zippo lighter. "You won't know if she was seeing anyone else, then?"

"Dear me, no. Nothing to do with me, anyway, was it? And we were never, er, intimate." Dalmer puffed on his pipe again. "You're seeking her killer in an attempt to clear your name obviously?"

"What?" Joe frowned. His thoughts had been far away. "Oh, yes. See, there was no sign of a struggle, no sign of a forced entry. That means she knew her killer. The only hint we have is a dating agency in Sanford."

"Have you spoken to them?"

Joe took a final drag on his cigarette and crushed it out in the ashtray as he stood up. "Not yet. And I don't know if they'll talk to me anyway." He smiled gruffly. "That won't stop me asking, mind. I'll catch you later, Stewart."

Chapter Six

With Lee busy in the kitchens, Joe opened up the Lazy Luncheonette at six, as usual, and cast a mean Monday morning eye out on the world at large.

Despite his victory at the Miner's Arms on Friday evening, he had had a bad weekend. A visit to Sanford Dating Agency on Saturday afternoon had proven fruitless for the simple reason that the place was closed. The police would not let him anywhere near Letty's home, and lacking any other investigative direction, he had been reduced to sitting in his flat above the café, brooding on all that had happened. He was in no better mood on Sunday, when he joined Lee and his wife, Cheryl and young son, Danny, for lunch. He had spoken to both Sheila and Brenda on the telephone, but other than that, he chose to hide away from the world.

By the time the two women joined him at the café on Monday morning, his temper was practically explosive, and he vented it on the Sanford Brewery dray men when they began to troop in for breakfast. Sheila, Brenda and Lee did not rise to his venom, and he guessed they were indulging his frustration, and when he finally left the café at 9.30am, he felt their relief.

Stepping out of the café, glancing across the dual carriageway to the access road of Doncaster Road Industrial Estate, he could see a dark blue Peugeot parked outside Broadbent's Auto Repairs. It had been there all weekend, its occupant a thirty-something woman, with a shower of flaming red hair. Joe did not know her, but he guessed she was from the press.

Shoving two fingers up at her, he made his way to the rear of Britannia Parade, climbed into his car and made for the town centre.

The Sanford Dating Agency was located in a row of rundown shops and offices near the market. Not only a dating agency, Joe learned, but a secretarial service, too. Finding the place still closed and locked up, he wandered onto the market.

Temperatures had risen a degree or two, taking away most of the ice which had covered the pavements for the last week, and yet the day remained sunny, but bitterly cold.

As a boy he recalled some two to three hundred stalls on Sanford market, selling everything from toys to clothing to shoes, to household goods, as well as the staple fruit, veg and bread. The passing of the years, ever-increasing stall rents, tighter trading rules and stiff competition from High Street discount shops like Poundland, had seen the market reduced to perhaps a hundred stalls, many of them dealing in second hand goods.

One such belonged to Mort Norris. He had rented the stall in the southeast corner of Sanford market for as long as Joe could remember, his merchandise a mishmash of china ornaments, household bric-a-brac, record players, video recorders, out of date computers, books and magazines.

"No money about, mate," he complained when Joe paused to pass the time with him.

Rolling a cigarette and lighting it, Joe did his best to sympathise. "It's the same all over, Mort. Lotta my customers are taking a butty for breakfast instead of the full monty." He blew a cloud of smoke into the sparkling air. "I thought you do better when money is tight. Second hand stuff, and that."

"Normally, yeah, but this time..." Mort shrugged. "Everyone's hanging on to every last penny." Mort too, lit a cigarette. "Cops dropped the charges yet, have they?"

"There are no charges. That's what I was telling you all on

Friday night. They questioned me cos I was one of the last people to see Letty alive. Hey, talking of her, what time does that dating agency open?" Joe pointed across the market square to the parade where Sanford Dating Agency stood.

"When she feels like it, Joe. Seen her come rolling in at one in the afternoon sometimes. Times are hard, buddy, and I reckon a business like hers could go under easy as anything. I meanersay, who's gonna pay twenty-five nicker to register with her, and then ten nicker for an intro when you can go down the pub and meet some bird for nothing?"

Joe smiled and puffed on his cigarette. "You get to meet a better class of woman for your twenty-five sovs."

Mort laughed harshly. "Better class of woman? Do me a favour. Not if she's taking on easy pickings like Letty Hill."

Joe was surprised. "You knew her? You said you didn't on Friday night."

A woman stopped at the stall and studied a second hand vacuum cleaner on sale at £20.

"Won't get a better deal than that on a Monday morning, luv," Mort told her.

With a sour glance at him, she moved on.

"Miserable cow." Mort shrugged himself deeper into his quilted topcoat and turned back to Joe. "Did I know Letty? Not well, and not in that way. I mean, jeez, Joe, I'm a married man. But she'd been round the block a few times. She was going out with Stewart Dalmer sometime last year, and George Robson was sniffing round it at one bit." He nodded in the direction of the dating agency. "Shouldna thought she was signed up with them. Shouldna thought she'd need to be."

"She had their card on her mantelpiece," Joe replied. "And you just said she was with them."

Mort shrugged again. "No, it was you who said it. You were talking about Letty and you asked when the dating shop was open."

"Did I?" Joe paused to wonder at the complex path Mort's

mind had followed. "Yeah, but... Oh, never mind. I could go nuts talking to someone like you."

Mort was not listening. He was concentrating on a customer studying a china shepherd boy. "Meissen that, missus. Won't get better for a fiver."

"Isn't it a bit cheap for Meissen?" she asked.

"Tiny chip on the base, luv. It's at the back so no one'll notice. You having it, are you?"

The woman passed him the ornament and he wrapped it in tissue, handed it over and took her five-pound note.

While this was going on, Joe glanced around in time to see a head of red hair disappear behind a carpet stall on the end of the aisle. He felt his gorge rising again.

"Another satisfied customer."

Mort's announcement brought Joe back from the mystery reporter. "Meissen? Come off it, Mort. I don't pass a bacon sandwich off as fillet steak."

"Did I say Meissen? I meant Mason. Wholesalers in Stoke-on-Trent. Went bust about three years ago and I got a job lot of their bankrupt stock." Mort grinned after the woman's departing back. "She'll stick it in a cabinet at home, then the next time The Antiques Roadshow is in town, she'll have it valued and find out it's worth about thirty bob. By then, it'll be too late to come back to me and complain."

Joe laughed. "You're a bloody conman, Mort."

"A businessman, Joe. Flannel gets you anywhere."

A familiar head of red hair, softer, shorter this time, made its way along the square of streets surrounding the market, and caught Joe's eye.

"There's my niece. I'll see y'around, Mort."

Joe made his way through the maze of stalls and came out opposite the dating agency, where Gemma was trying the door.

"No one home," he said. "I tried once."

Gemma greeted him with a cold smile. "Morning, Uncle

Joe. I figured you'd be here sometime today. I spoke to the woman on the phone last Friday and she promised she'd be here for ten o'clock."

Joe checked his watch. "Only five to." He glanced around and his eyes lighted on a large supermarket on the southwest corner. "What say we grab a cup of tea and come back in ten minutes?"

Gemma nodded.

The supermarket suffered from the Monday morning vacuum as much as the rest of town. Staff busied themselves filling shelves and freezers, managers strode self-importantly around the food hall, talking with their crew, pointing out empty shelves in need of filling, pinning up notices of special offers here and there. But customers were in short supply. There was no queue in the café either, where Joe asked for two teas while Gemma took a table by the windows.

"It's self-service, sir," the assistant told Joe.

"Yes, I know. So I'm forming a one-man queue, waiting for service."

The young man shook his head. "No, sir. You take a teapot and fill it yourself from the hot water machine." He gestured at a machine bearing a range of buttons which dispensed several kinds of coffee and boiling water for tea.

Grumbling to himself, Joe took two individual metal teapots, put one of them under the outlet, and pressed the button for hot water. When the pot was filled, he stared into clear, boiling water.

"There's no teabag in here," he said.

The assistant, his frustration rising, too, explained, "Some people prefer speciality teas, so you have to check whether you have a teabag in the pot."

His temper rising again, Joe put the pot to one side and while the second filled, he checked other teapots for contents. "You know the word service, as in self-service? Did they skip that bit when they thought of this place?"

"I'm only doing my job, sir," the lad replied. "As I was taught on my training course."

Joe moved along to the checkout. "You had training?"

"Two days." The assistant took Joe's money and rang it up. "You've obviously never been here before."

"Why would I? I run a café on Doncaster Road. When I do eat elsewhere, it's usually in pubs or proper restaurants, not alleged fast food places. You want to get on in catering, lad, this is not the place to learn."

"I don't want to get on in catering. I took this job because it was the only one I could get with my degree."

Joe's eyebrows rose. "You have a degree?

"Astrophysics."

With a shake of the head, Joe took his teapots away. "A degree in astrophysics and you end up serving in a dump like this? What a waste of taxpayers' money."

"I agree," the youngster said, "but there aren't that many vacancies for astrophysicists in Sanford."

Joe moved to the cutlery rack, collected tiny portions of milk and sachets of sugar, and then frowned again.

"Hey, Einstein, there are no teaspoons here."

The young man, his features as flushed as his smart, mauve uniform, came over, and pulled out a wooden stirrer. "We don't use teaspoons, sir. These are cheaper, they cut down on washing up, and people don't steal them."

Joe's face crumpled to a familiar scowl. "You know, son, I had the misfortune to be married once. The missus dragged me all over Europe. It was sheer hell, but I'll say this for it: everywhere I went, when I ordered tea or coffee, it was served by a waiter or waitress, and I got a spoon with it." He reached into one of the other drawers and took out a knife. "I refuse to stir my tea with a wooden stick."

The youngster scowled back. "I don't suppose there's any point reminding you to please clear the table, either."

"Am I the customer or an employee?"

"We ask that customers clear away after them."

"And then what? You want me to mop the floors?" Joe picked up his tray. "If I asked the truckers in my place to clean up after them, do you know what they'd say? Trust me, lad, the kind of language they would use doesn't come into your debates on galaxies… or your two day training course."

He crossed the café and sat opposite his niece.

"Sorry I took so long. Apparently they don't understand the principles of serving customers."

Gemma smiled and took a cup and teapot. "I heard. Don't tell me you didn't know how these places work."

"Rumour only," Joe replied filling his cup and stirring in milk and sugar with the handle of the knife. "Like I told sonny Jim, I think the only times I've ever been into one of these places it's been with Sheila or Brenda, and they dealt with the counter hands." He sipped the tea. "Ugh. Cheap teabags, too."

Gemma was surprised. "You can tell the difference?"

"I've spent all my life in the business. I can tell." Pushing his cup to one side, he took out his tobacco tin and began to roll a cigarette. "So bring me up to speed. Have you learned anything over the weekend?"

The counter assistant, passing on his rounds, ensuring everything was as it should be, spotted Joe's cigarette equipment. "Excuse me, sir, but you can't smoke in here. It's illegal."

Joe licked the paper and finished rolling the cigarette. He gestured at Gemma. "This is Detective Sergeant Craddock of the Sanford Police. She's here to make sure crumblies like me don't get hassle from young kids. I'm not going to smoke it in here. Now be a good lad and bugger off back to your counter and dream of the day when a white dwarf is gonna smash into my café and shut me down."

While the lad wandered off, Joe tucked the cigarette in the top pocket of his gilet, and raised his eyebrows at Gemma.

"We're right at the beginning of the investigation, Uncle Joe," Gemma said, "so we don't know much yet. Her neighbours neither saw nor heard anything… oh, except for one neighbour who swears she heard a car pull up outside Letty's place around one in the morning. It didn't leave again until about two."

"But she didn't see anyone get in or out of the car?"

"Nope. Just glanced through the bedroom curtains as it arrived and thought she heard it leave again an hour later."

"It was the killer, obviously."

"Possibly," Gemma corrected.

"Come on, Gemma, you don't still think it was me, do you?"

"I never thought it was you, Uncle Joe. I'm sure Vickers doesn't believe it, either. But right now, you're the last confirmed contact we have for the woman, and we're trying to piece together her final hours. That's why I'm talking to Angela Foster."

About to drink from his cup, Joe paused. "Who?"

"Angela Foster. She runs the dating agency."

A shadow loomed over the table; Joe looked up into the podgy eyes of a mean security man. "Help you?"

For all his glower, the security guard maintained a respectful tone. "We've had a complaint from a member of staff that you've been giving him verbal abuse, sir."

"I've been educating him in the correct method of catering for customers," Joe argued.

"We have a policy, whereby we do not tolerate abuse of our staff… sir."

"And I have a policy that says I prefer to be served rather than employed," Joe countered.

"In that case, may I suggest you take your custom elsewhere?" The thin deference disappeared altogether. "Before we chuck you out."

Gemma dug into her bag and took out her warrant card.

"Detective Sergeant Craddock, Sanford CID. Do you understand the difference between escorting someone from the building and throwing them out? One is legitimate, the other constitutes assault. Mr Murray is with me, and he will leave when I'm ready to go."

Hands held up in a gesture of surrender, the security man stepped back and turned to leave.

"And you can tell your bosses if they put spoons out instead of wooden sticks... oh, for crying out loud. How could I have been so blind?" He faced Gemma, his features urgent. "Do you have those photographs with you? The ones you showed me on Friday?" When she nodded and reached for her briefcase, he pressed on, "The one taken in the kitchen. Let me see it."

Opening the briefcase, Gemma took out the folder and sifted through the images, found the one he wanted, and passed it to him.

Joe scrutinised it closely, his practised eye looking for what he already knew was not there. Cup and saucer in the plastic drainer, a half empty bottle of washing up liquid sitting in a small basket to one side of the sink, but...

"See," he said, turning the photograph towards Gemma. "No spoon."

She frowned. "What about it?"

Joe sighed. "What have I always taught you about human nature, Gemma? We're creatures of habit. Now think about the times when you make a cup of tea at home... you do make the odd cup of tea, don't you? Or do you leave it to Paul all the time?"

"No. I make cups of tea."

"Right, so you get out a cup, saucer and a spoon, don't you?"

Gemma considered this for a moment. "Well, maybe Letty didn't take milk. Maybe she didn't take milk or sugar. She wouldn't need a spoon then, would she?"

"Oh yes she would." Joe gestured at the photograph again. "There's no teapot. Whoever made that cuppa, it was done with the teabag in the cup, not in a pot, and he – or she – would have needed a spoon to get the teabag out. And anyway, I happen to know that Letty did take milk. I did spend Wednesday night there. This wasn't Letty. When this cup of tea was made, Letty was already dead. Or do you think she made him a brew without making one for herself and then washed hers up before he murdered her? No, Gemma, this was the killer. He was doing something in that house after he killed Letty, and he felt secure enough to make himself a cup of tea while he was doing it."

"And you think a missing spoon points at it. He may have washed the spoon and put it back in the kitchen drawer."

"Then why didn't he do the same with the cup and saucer? The spoon is important, but I don't know why." Joe's brow knitted. "Lemme see those other pictures, will you? The ones of the living room."

Gemma once more rifled through the photographs and handed over two or three images. Joe, too, sorted through them until he came across the one where the display cabinet was prominent.

Chewing his lip, he shook his head. "No. It's there."

"What?" Gemma demanded. "What's there?"

Again Joe half turned the photograph so she could see, and pointed to the shelf below the one on which his rose was visible. "A set of Regency spoons in a velvet covered case. I was talking to Letty about them on Wednesday night. They're worth about five hundred pounds. I wondered whether the cheeky sod had nicked them and used one to stir his tea while he was doing whatever he was doing after he killed her. Obviously not. They're still in place."

"I can get Scientific Support to check. If they've been moved, the dust in the cabinet will show it."

Joe gave a wry, wrinkled smile. "They have been moved.

Letty took them out of the cabinet on Wednesday night to show me."

Gemma's shoulders slumped again. After a moment's thought, she brightened up. "I can get the dreaded SS to check the cup, though."

Joe was puzzled. "But it's been washed up."

Warming to her task, Gemma said, "I'm gonna do an Uncle Joe here, and speculate. Our man leaves no dabs. We know that much. Let's assume he uses latex gloves, like those we use to avoid contaminating a crime scene. He would take those off to wash the cup and saucer. Right?"

"Because if he didn't they'd maybe end up slipping off and he may accidentally leave one behind? Yeah, okay."

"They're not close fitting, Joe. They could easily come off when wet. So, he takes them off to wash the cup and saucer. He may just have left a partial on the cup handle."

"Wouldn't your dab men have already tested it?"

"They may have done, they may not. I'll look into it when I get back to the station. Course, our man could have used kitchen gloves and taken them with him, so it might lead nowhere."

Joe considered this. "Did Scientific Support analyse the residue in the cup?"

"Hmm." Gemma nodded as she finished off her tea. "Water, some traces of detergent. Nothing else. At least, not yet." She checked through the window, and a brunette opening up the doors of the Sanford Dating Agency. "Hey up, Angie's here."

Joe gulped down his tea and stood up. "Let's go, then."

Gemma made to pick up the tray, but Joe stopped her.

"Are you a customer or an employee?"

She picked up the tray. "Neither. I'm a copper and I have to put on a show for community relations."

Chapter Seven

As they crossed the market square, making for the dating agency, Joe once more spotted the flowing head of red hair, but this time, he made out a freckled face and a shapely body clothed in a black skirt and dark, quilted topcoat. A compact camera was pressed to her eye, aimed in his direction.

"Rosemary Ecclesfield," Gemma said. "Reporter for the *Sanford Gazette*. Complete cow. Watch the reports, Uncle Joe, or she'll crucify you, and she won't let trivia like the truth get in the way."

"I know the editor," Joe promised. "Come on. Let's talk to this other woman, Angie wossname."

Angela Foster was aged about fifty, according to Joe's estimate. A pretty woman, broad in the beam and bust, with a flowing head of natural brunette hair and a pleasant humour showing through her brown eyes. Dressed in a conservative, dark blue business suite, the skirt covering her chunky knees, she greeted Gemma with a warm smile, Joe with uncertainty.

"Isn't he the one who's been arrested for the murder?" she asked.

"Don't believe everything you read in the papers, Mrs Foster," Gemma said with a glance back at Rosemary Ecclesfield on the market. "Mr Murray was one of the last people to see Letty alive, so we questioned him, but he is not a suspect. Quite the opposite, in fact. He's helping us with the inquiry."

Angela was not quite satisfied. "Helping with the inquiry? Isn't that the same as being a suspect?"

"No," Joe reassured her. "Letty was alive and well when I last saw her. What Gemma means is, I'm a private investigator."

Now Angela's eyebrows shot up. "No you're not. You own that lorry drivers café on Doncaster Road. The Lazy something or other."

"The Lazy Luncheonette; where we make sure the drivers have spoons to stir their tea," Joe responded. "Listen, lady, we just want to know what you know about Letty Hill."

Angela led them into a small shop-like area. Where Joe might have expected a couple of people working at word processors or answering the phone, there was no one. Most of the floor space was taken up with a large photocopier/collator, the overhead shelves were stacked with packs of paper of varying sizes and quality, and powder cartridges for the copier, and laser printer refills. Several box files filled one corner of the shelving, and behind the computer, sitting on the solitary desk to the back of the service counter, was brightly coloured, point of sale material advertising the Sanford Dating Agency and its associated services.

Angela ushered them through the counter to the desk, drew up a couple of stiff-backed chairs for them and invited them to sit, while she flopped into her executive, tilt and turn seat and switched on the computer.

While she fussed and tutted, kicking off her winter boots and slipping her feet into a pair of sensible flats, Joe looked out through the dusty window onto the market, where sunshine gave a false impression of spring warmth. The impression was belied by the few shoppers who had braved the cold, wrapped up in warm coats and scarves, hoods raised, caps pulled low. For Joe, it mirrored the topsy-turvy events of the last few days. While everything appeared as normal, the undertone told a different tale.

Angela's voice brought him back to the interior of the Sanford Dating Agency office. "I know nothing of Letty Hill.

And while I don't mind talking to the police, I'm not sure I have to answer your questions."

With a good deal more patience than Joe, Gemma explained, "Mr Murray's powers of observation are without equal, Mrs Foster. If you don't answer him, I'll only ask the same question, and you'll have to answer me. Now, please humour us for the time being. No one is accusing you of anything, but we do need some background information on Letty."

Again Angela shrugged. "I just told you, I know nothing about her. I was surprised when you rang and said she was one of my members. I checked over the weekend, and I'm afraid she's never been registered with my agency."

Joe frowned. "But she had your business card."

"It's not difficult to get hold of, Mr Murray. For all I know, one of her friends or neighbours may have given it to her."

"She wasn't registered with you as a temp, then?" Gemma asked. "A secretary?"

"It's not that kind of secretarial agency, Sergeant. I don't employ others. I carry out the work myself. That's why I'm not always in the office. I visit and work with people who need short term secretarial assistance."

"Short term as in a few days?" Joe asked.

"Less than that," Angela admitted. "Usually it's just a morning or an afternoon. And when I do come back here, it's normally to prepare and print the work out."

Gemma was about to say something, but Joe beat her to it. "What kind of clients?"

"All sorts. Tradesmen who need a VAT or tax appeal typing up, local authors, artists who may need some publicity material putting together. Right now I'm typing up a manuscript for a local historian. He's thinking of publishing it at his own expense, and I'm hoping he'll allow me to do the formatting."

"I'm surprised you don't work from home," Joe

commented.

Angela pointed to the large photocopier and other machinery. "I don't have room for those in my living room."

"Must be a paying game to afford a place like this." Joe raised his hands and eyes to the office around them.

"I own the office, Mr Murray, I don't rent it. In fact I own the building. It was my grandfather's print shop."

Again Gemma tried to get a word in, but Joe was faster. "So where does the dating agency fit in?"

"A sideline, I suppose you could call it," Angela replied. "I was divorced about twenty years ago, and I learned what a problem it was meeting other people, so I started up the Sanford Dating Agency."

"And you interview potential members here?"

Angie shook her head. "Occasionally, but most of it is done online, these days."

"How much do you charge?" Joe demanded.

"Uncle Joe, if I could get a word in…" Gemma allowed a pause to let her protest sink in. Angela looked suspiciously from one to the other. "We're drifting off the point, here."

"He's your uncle?" Angela asked. The hint of suspicion turned to direct challenge. "What's going on here? You, let me see your identification."

The demand was aimed at Gemma, who tutted and took out her warrant card.

"There's nothing going on, Mrs Foster," Joe assured the woman. "Gemma is my niece, but she's also the senior CID officer in Sanford. And Gemma, you're wrong, this is all to the point." He turned on Angela again. "You say Letty is not on your books, we believe she was. There is a possibility that she met her killer through your agency. You're telling me that your business is done mostly online. How closely do you check members' backgrounds?"

Angela's ears coloured slightly. "Well, I do what I can, naturally."

"But that's not a lot, is it, without paying for a criminal records check, and that would cost more than the twenty-five quid you charge for registration."

"They pay by credit card, Mr Murray," Angela protested. "Anyone who has a credit card must be above board or the card companies would spot them."

"I can get a credit card in a different name like that." Joe snapped his fingers. "Lemme ask you whether you check the names on the payments to see if they match the names on the application."

This time Angela's cheeks blushed a furious crimson.

"In other words, anyone can sign up as long as they pay." Joe chewed spit.

"You think Cassons over in Leeds do any different?" Angela snapped. "They're just the same, only larger. I'll tell you again; Letty Hill was not a member of my agency."

"As far as you know."

"I checked—"

"Let's all calm down," Gemma interrupted. "Uncle Joe, are you saying that it's possible for people to give Mrs Foster a false name and still become members?"

"Exactly," Joe declared. "Look, I run a café. I deal in cash, not credit cards. Just suppose I did. I'd have hundreds of transactions every day. Do you think I'd have time to scrutinise them all? My interest would be the amount, nothing else. Now take a busy woman like Mrs Foster, here. Does she have the time to check them all? Well, maybe, but what about when she's busy with manuscripts for local historians? She's working to a deadline. She's notified of the transaction. Is the amount right? Yes it is. Good. Back to Sanford's role in the Battle of New Orleans. The reference number is probably the member's number, too. So that's all you need. Am I right, Mrs Foster?"

Angela said nothing; merely nodded.

"You're not doing anything wrong, lady," Joe reassured her.

"Administratively iffy, sure, but what the hell, we all cut corners. But it does provide an opening for our Valentine Strangler."

"But if Letty Hill isn't a member..." Gemma trailed off, her face lined in deep thought. "Mrs Foster, can you interrogate the database by address?"

Angela nodded. "I've never had to do it, but the software says it can be done."

Gemma took out her pocketbook. "Would you try, please? Thirty-three Oakleigh Grove."

While Angela tapped speculatively at the keyboard, her lips pursed, eyes burning with a fire of fine concentration, Joe took one of her leaflets and read through the pluses of joining a dating agency.

"Something I've never tried," he muttered under his breath.

Angela looked up from the screen. "Sorry, Mr Murray?"

"Nothing, nothing. Just check this address for us."

Angela went back to her concentrated effort. A moment later her eyes lit again. She typed hurriedly at the keyboard, hit the return key and sat back looking at the screen, satisfaction spread across her face.

"I told you. Nothing." She turned the monitor to face Gemma.

Gemma checked it and frowned. "You've spelled it wrong, Mrs Foster." With a frown, Gemma pointed to where Angela had typed in *Oakliegh*. "It's O-A-K-L-*E-I*-G-H."

"I hope your secretarial work is better than that," Joe grumbled, still reading through the leaflet.

Angela blushed. "My secretarial output is proofread several times, Mr Murray." She typed again. This time her face lit in surprise. "Oh. That's odd."

Joe put down the leaflet and along with Gemma leaned closer. "What?"

"We have member living at 33 Oakleigh Grove, certainly, but it's not Letty Hill. It's a woman named Letitia Collina."

"Letty is short for Letitia, and Letitia is her proper name," Joe declared. "Dunno where she got Collina from. Can we see a picture?"

Angela clicked on the link and the screen flicked over to the member's page, from where a photograph of Letty Hill smiled at the camera.

"That's her," Gemma said right away. "Mrs Foster, do you keep a track on introductions?"

"Of course. People pay for introductions, so I have to ensure they're not sent to the same man twice."

"Could you print off a list of all the introductions Letty took?"

Angela looked askance. "It'll take a good few minutes." She checked the screen. "She joined three years ago, there's been no activity for the last year and a half. All her details are likely to be archived."

"If you could," Gemma urged. "We have very little to go on, and although this is a bit thin, it may just take us somewhere."

"Thin is right," Joe said, watching Angela as she began to interrogate the database again. "You really need to check whether any of the other victims are registered with Mrs Foster."

"All in good time, Uncle Joe."

He grunted and rolled a cigarette while Angela kept one beady eye on him.

He was about to warn her off, tell her that he knew he could not smoke it in her office, when a thought struck him. "Mrs Foster, how does the system work?"

"The computer system? I don't know. I bought the software off the web."

"Not the bloody computer system. I mean the dating system. How do you set up a meeting between two people?"

Still tapping away at the computer, Angela gave half a mind to Joe. "It's quite simple. They ring in, or more often than not, email, asking for an introduction. I search the database looking for someone who meets at least some of their requirements, they pay me, and I send the web details along to them so they can get in touch."

"Right, so you've made the introduction. Is that where your job ends?"

"Yes. At least that part of it. There have been one or two weddings come from introductions and I was invited to them." She smiled dreamily. "It's nice when that happens."

"If you'd introduced me to my wife, I really would be the Valentine Strangler, but it'd be you I was strangling."

Angela hit a key and across the room, a laser printer began to run A4 sheets through its innards.

"Really, Mr Murray, that's not a very nice attitude."

"She wasn't a very nice woman," Joe argued.

Gemma laughed. "Let's leave Aunt Alison out of this, Joe. What were you getting at?"

"Just this. Suppose Mrs Foster introduced Letty to Mr X, say, two years ago. Suppose Letty and Mr X had a couple of dates, and took matters no further. Suppose then, Mr X got in touch with Letty last week." Joe looked at Angela. "That would be nothing to do with you, would it?"

"Absolutely nothing," Angela agreed. "I could have introduced them ten years ago, if they were both members, but if they came together again last week, it would be none of my business."

"So what are you getting at, Uncle Joe?"

"You really need to check all four victims and you'll have to go back a long way. Back to when they joined the agency, if they are members." He waved at the laser printer. "You could have reams of paper to go through."

Gemma shrugged. "Vickers will insist on it. Mrs Foster, what kind of dating advice do you give your members?"

"The correct advice, of course. We say to them all, when you're meeting a man – or woman – for the first time, make sure it's in a public place."

"But you don't actually arrange the meeting?" Gemma persisted.

"No. Good Lord, if I had to go to that trouble, the agency wouldn't be worth it. I only make pennies out of it, you know."

Joe picked up Gemma's train of thought. "So in practice, they could go back to her place or his on the first date."

"They're adults, Mr Murray, not children. They're free to do whatever they wish. I give them advice, but if they want to ignore that advice, it's their choice."

"And I know for sure that Letty was not fussy about inviting first dates back to her place." Joe chewed his lip as he met Gemma's eyes. "This entire line of enquiry could be running you up a gum tree."

"Like missing spoons? We've nothing else to go on, Joe. We're certain this man – we assume it's a man – doesn't pick his victims at random. He knows something about them in advance, and the agency's card is the first hint of a new line of enquiry."

Angela crossed to the printer and collected up three sheets of A4; returning to her seat, she handed them to Gemma. "Do you have the names and addresses of the other ladies?"

Gemma put the freshly printed sheets into briefcase, and took out a folder.

Over the next half hour they checked the other three victims using their names and addresses, but only one, Fiona Temple, showed on Angela's database, and the agency had not heard from her for over five years.

"She's been dead three years," Joe pointed out.

"She'd been a member for four years before that," Angela countered.

"Print us off her details, then," Gemma ordered. "Mrs Foster, if these other two women were not with your agency, who else would they go to?"

"Plenty of sites on the web, but the really big one round here is Cassons in Leeds. They're more expensive than me. They have big, fancy offices, just off City Square, and they offer a full matrimonial service. But I don't think they're any better than me. One of my male clients said he'd been with them, and they were sending him introductions for women who lived as far away as Ripon and Thirsk."

Joe grunted. "Long way to travel for a legover."

His remark prompted further disapproval from Angela. Striking the key to send instructions to the printer, she lectured him. "Sex is not the be all and end all of a relationship, Mr Murray. There's companionship, too."

"Not in Letty Hill's case." Before Angela could pick him up again, Joe asked, "Have you ever dated any of your male members?"

She glowered. "Mind your own bloody business."

Joe backed off. "All right, all right, don't tie your suspenders up. I was only asking." Joe fished into his pocket and drew out his battered, brown leather wallet. "Here: let me leave you with one of the STAC cards."

Angela stared suspiciously at him. "Stack?"

"STAC. S-T-A-C. It's short for the Sanford 3rd Age Club. I'm Chairman. We charge about the same as you, but we hold weekly get-togethers at the Miner's Arms and regular outings at attractive prices. The only stipulation is you have to be at least fifty years old."

"I don't qualify," Angela retorted.

Joe almost replied, 'you could have fooled me', but bit his tongue just in time. "We're not rigid on it. Keep the card and if you change your mind, ring me, Sheila or Brenda on any of those numbers."

Angela put the card to one side and crossed to the printer where she gathered up the sheets for Gemma.

"I think that's all for the time being, Mrs Foster. Thank you for your help." Gemma put the sheets away, locked up her briefcase, rose from her seat, and shook hands. "You ready, Uncle Joe?"

"Just a minute, Gemma." Skimming through one of Angela's leaflets, Joe gave the woman a crooked smile. "If I joined your agency, how soon would you send me the first introduction?"

She appeared shocked. "I'm sorry, Mr Murray, but I couldn't accept you."

"Why not? I'm single and over twenty-one."

"You're also a suspect in a murder inquiry."

Gemma giggled and Joe fumed.

"I am not a suspect."

"You're also quite bad-tempered. I wouldn't want any of my lady members coming back to me complaining about your irritability."

"I am not bad-tempered," Joe snapped.

"Yes you are. You're losing your temper now because you can't get your own way."

Joe sucked in his breath and forced himself to calm down. "I am irritable, yes, but I get out of bed at five every morning, and I work like a dog. I don't have the luxury of saying, 'sod it, I'll have a day off', and I can't laze around home until ten in the morning. Granted, I am outspoken, but that's nothing fresh in this town."

Angela remained firm. "I'm sorry, Mr Murray. I don't like turning business away, but I have to think of my other members. Now, if you'll excuse me, I must get on."

Still smarting from her refusal, Joe tucked the leaflet in his pocket, and followed Gemma out into the cold sunshine. "Your next move?" he asked.

Gemma shrugged. "I'll get someone in Leeds to follow up on Cassons, and I'll pass this stuff onto the team. They can do the donkey work on them."

"I'd better get back to work," Joe said, lighting the cigarette he had rolled. "Don't forget to check on that spoon business."

"I'll get the message to Des Kibble."

Joe frowned. "Who?"

"Des Kibble. He's one of the Crime Scene Investigators from Wakefield. Fingerprint specialist. Supposedly one of the best. If anyone can crack it, it's him." Gemma pecked him on the cheek. "I'll see you later, Uncle Joe."

Chapter Eight

His route back to the Lazy Luncheonette took Joe past the spread of Sanford Memorial Park, a large, open expanse of greenery offsetting the dour, former industrial landscape of the town.

He noticed a team of council employees hard at work, dragging dead wood to a mobile crusher, and amongst them, he could clearly make out the burly figure of George Robson shouting orders to the younger men in the team.

Ignoring the double yellow lines outside the park gates, Joe pulled into the kerb, and the dark Peugeot which had followed him from the town carried on past. As he climbed out, he saw Rosemary Ecclesfield pull in further along the road.

Ignoring her, he hurried into the park and across to the workers. "Hey up, George," he shouted above the deafening roar of the machine. "How long have you been the ganger?"

George lifted his ear protectors and shouted over the cacophony. "Since they sent a team of kids here. I'm one of the few trained to work with this machine." He waved at the crusher where the younger men fed sawn-off branches and twigs into the hopper while others stood at the far end where the shredded product emerged into large sacks, some of it as fine as sawdust. "And I don't get any extra dosh for it, you know, but if we left it to these noddies, they'd end up jamming their arm in the bleeding thing. What's cooking, anyway, Joe? Have plod let it all drop, yet?"

"Officially, no, unofficially, yes. I've just been to the Sanford Dating Agency."

George grinned. "Angie Foster." He smacked his lips. "Tasty. And a right little raver when you get a few Bacardis inside her."

Joe puffed agitatedly on his cigarette. "That's not how she tells it. Comes across as more of a right little miss prim."

"Well, she would, wouldn't she?" George turned on the young men, one of whom was trying to free a jam in the machinery. "Hey, you, dipstick, are you trying to lose your arm? Turn the bloody thing off while you clear out the hopper."

"Yeah, well, I just thought—"

"If you were capable of thinking, I could nip to the Fettlers for a pint. Turn it off." As near silence fell, George turned his attention back to Joe. "Sorry, mate. What was I saying. Oh, yeah, Angie. Hot as one of your bacon butties, Joe."

Joe blew out another lungful of smoke. "Hot as Letty Hill?"

George laughed. "Letty? You've gotta be joking. My freezer is hotter than her."

"Hotter than she was," Joe corrected. "She's dead, remember."

"Yeah, well, you know what I meant. I took her out coupla times last year, when she was on the bounce from toffee-nose, Dalmer. No go, man. And if I can't get to first base, no man can."

"I did," Joe argued.

"She was drunk, wasn't she?"

"Was she hell as like dru… Look, it doesn't matter. According to Mort Norris, Letty had been round the block more times than a number eight bus."

"He's been listening to Dalmer spinning the tale," George swore. "For a so-called historian, Dalmer dreams up more fairy stories than Helmut Anderson."

"You mean Hans Christian Anderson."

"Whoever. Dalmer reckoned he'd had Letty and so many

other women, but it wasn't true. Teachers aren't allowed to get it on with their pupils, are they? He'd have been struck off or summat."

"I also didn't know Dalmer was a historian," Joe said, ignoring most of George's comment. "I thought he taught English."

"Did he? I thought he had this sideline in history."

"Antiques, you donk."

"Well I knew it was summat old. Mort Norris knows him better than me." At the sound of the machinery starting up again, George put his ear protectors back on and raised his voice above the cacophony. "Take it from me, Joe, Letty Hill was one of the original vestment virgins." He pointed at Joe's car. "And you'd better get a move on. Vinny Gillespie's over there, ready to give you a ticket."

Joe looked back at the park entrance where PC Gillespie could be seen walking round the parked car. With a gasped, "Thanks, George," Joe ran for the gates. "Vinny. Wait, Vinny. I'm here."

"Oh it's you, Mr Murray," Gillespie said as Joe arrived. "You know you really shouldn't be parked here."

"Yeah, yeah, I know," Joe apologised. "I'm sorry, kid. I was following up a lead on the Letty Hill business."

Gillespie features darkened. "Oh, yeah. I was sorry to hear about that; you getting pulled in, like. It's this mob from Wakefield, you know. They don't know the people round here, so they're just treading on everyone's toes…" He looked worried. "You won't, er, you know, tell anyone I said that, will you?"

"Course not, Vinny." Joe eyed his car. "Long as you can look the other way while I get back in my car and drive off."

Gillespie grunted. "You wanna watch it, Mr Murray. I should book you, but I'll let it go. Not everyone's like me, though."

"Sure, kid." Joe hurried to the driver's seat, fumbling the

key in the lock. "Call in at the Lazy Luncheonette, sometime. We'll sort you out some tea or something."

Up ahead, he saw smoke come from the Peugeot's exhaust as Rosemary Ecclesfield also drove away.

Joe started the engine and drove away, half his mind relieved at having just missed a parking ticket, the other half ruminating on the information George had just given him.

"It's like I speak to three different people and I get three different Lettys," he said to his companions as he got back to the Lazy Luncheonette just before the lunchtime rush began.

"Nothing so strange about that, Joe," Sheila replied. "Look at yourself. If you asked the dray men, they'd probably say you were grumpy but amiable."

Never one to resist temptation, Brenda commented, "Whereas we'd just say you were a miserable old bugger."

"Bog off."

Joe checked his large metal teapot, sniffed it suspiciously, and tossed the teabags into the waste bin. Moving into the kitchen, squeezing past Lee's wife, Cheryl, he put the pot on the drainer for washing, and took down the replacements, which he swilled under the cold water.

As he stepped from the kitchen, back into the counter area, the café door trilled, opened and Rosemary Ecclesfield stepped in.

"Mr Murray—"

"Get out."

If Rosemary was taken aback by his bluntness, she soon recovered. "Fine way to treat customers."

"You're not a customer. You're a reporter, and you're not welcome. Now get out before I throw you out."

She did not move. "I want—"

"You write in English, so presumably you can understand it when it's spoken. For the last time, get out."

"Joe—"

He cut Sheila off as abruptly as he had done Rosemary.

"What is so complicated about get out? It's two simple words, and they mean turn round, go back to the gutter you crawled out of."

"You're making a big mistake, Murray."

"Joe, for God's sake, what is wrong with you?" Brenda asked.

He pointed a shaking finger at Rosemary. "This... harridan has been following me all weekend. She was on the market this morning, she was at the Memorial Park when I spoke to George." He aimed his finger through the window at Broadbent's the other side of the dual carriageway. "She's been parked over there since that stupid TV broadcast on Friday. She's a muck-raker from the *Gazette*. Well, get this straight, lady: I have nothing to say to you, so clear off before I chase you off."

Rosemary's fiery eyes glowered. "You'll regret this."

With a roar, brandishing his metal teapot, Joe ran from behind the counter and rushed at her. She turned and beat a hasty retreat, leaving the café, and running away along the pavement.

Joe, his features flushed, returned, and took at the amazed stares of his staff and the few customers.

"If she comes here again, you tell her she's not welcome. Get her out."

"Joe, sit down and let me get you a cup of tea." Sheila's voice carried that air of authority which brooked no argument.

Joe obeyed, sitting at table five while Sheila relieved him of his teapot, and after leaving it with Brenda for her to finish preparing it, she returned with a beaker of strong, sweet tea.

"Joe—"

"Don't tell me how to run my business," he warned.

She remained firm. "I'm not interested in how you run the business. But I am interested in your health. For goodness' sake, Joe, your stress levels are somewhere above the roof. She may be a muck-raker, as you put it, but she's doing her job, and you're well within your rights to demand that she leave, but you don't go chasing after her like that. It damages no one but you."

Brenda left Cheryl to help Lee prepare lunches and sat with Joe. "Sheila is right, you know. That cow will slag you off all over the front pages for that. And all you can do is complain after the event."

Joe sipped at the tea. "I've a thick skin."

"You wouldn't have thought so," Sheila said. "I've never seen you so angry."

Joe slammed his beaker down. "Do you know how she's hassled me since Friday? Everywhere I turn, she's there taking pictures."

"And she hasn't spoken to you?" Brenda asked.

"Until just now, no."

Brenda's face became grim. "Ten to one she's concocting some acid against you. Have you thought of complaining to the editor? Following you like that, it could be construed as stalking."

"An invasion of privacy," Sheila agreed. As Joe reached for his mobile, she stopped him. "Finish your tea first, and calm down." She held his hand. "Joe, you brought Cheryl in to help out. Why don't you take some time off? Proper time off. Get away from the café for a few days. We can cope, and it will help you get things into perspective."

"Yeah. Yeah. Maybe you're right."

"Oh, and talking of time off, Brenda, I need to get away early this afternoon, if you don't mind."

Brenda nodded. "No problem, Sheila. Something on?"

"Stewart Dalmer is coming to look at some of my bits."

The inadvertent ambiguity of the statement made even Joe smile. "And I've been trying for years to get a look at your bits."

As if she suddenly realised what she had said, Sheila blushed. "I didn't mean that. I meant my knickknack... My ornaments."

Brenda's smile faded. They followed her gaze through the windows and across the road where Rosemary's car had pulled up, turned round and now parked outside Broadbent's facing towards them.

With a mean scowl, Joe picked up his mobile and ran through the directory before selecting the number of the *Sanford Gazette*. Listening to it ring out, he picked up his tea, and moved into and through the kitchen to stand out in the back yard.

"News desk."

"Gimme Ian Lofthouse."

"Who's calling?"

"Joe Murray, and tell him before he tries to cry off, I'll go to the Press Complaints Commission unless he speaks to me now."

"Well, I don't know—"

"Just do it, son, or you'll be in trouble, too."

The line went dead as he was put on hold. A few seconds later, Ian Lofthouse's soft voice came through.

"Hello, Joe. How are you, me old marrer?"

"Bloody annoyed is how I am, and it's down to you."

"Me?" Lofthouse sounded shocked. "What have I done, Joe?"

"Rosemary Ecclesfield, that's what."

Lofthouse groaned. "Oh. Her. I know she's following your arrest for the killing of that old bird last week. She's looking for the story, Joe. It's what she's paid for."

"I was not arrested," Joe insisted. "And your hack is not following the story, she's following me. Everywhere I turn, she's there. I've just chased her outta my place and now she's sitting on the industrial estate opposite, where, I might add, she's been all weekend. Get her off my back, Ian, or I'll lodge a complaint with either the PCC or the cops."

"Technically, Joe, she's not doing anything illegal."

"So you're telling me the stalking rules only apply to politicians and celebrities? How many years have we known each other?"

"I know."

"And how much advertising has the *Gazette* had off me?"

"Er, as far as I know, none. You don't advertise that place of yours. You always reckon you don't need to."

"I mean the Sanford 3rd Age Club," Joe snapped. "We spend a fair few bob with you every year, Ian, especially when we're looking for new members, so don't flannel me. Get this bag off me."

"Joe, please listen. She's looking for the story. That's all. And she won't get anything really rough past me. If she comes on too strong, I'll tone it down. Give her an interview."

"I can't, and you know I can't. The police may not really suspect me, but I have been questioned and if I talk to the press, it could blow the whole case wide open, and then the cops would have me for trying to pervert the course of justice… or something. Just get her away from me. I find her following me again, I won't be responsible."

Lofthouse sighed. "All right, Joe. Leave it with me. I'll see what I can do, but I'm telling you now, she's a law unto herself… or, at least she thinks she is. Ambitious, you know. She won't let go that easily."

Joe killed the connection, rolled a cigarette, marched through the kitchen, and out through the front doors. Lighting his cigarette, he leaned against the brick gap between his windows and Patel's Minimarket, his eyes narrowed on Rosemary's car. Taking a long drag on the cigarette, he let out the smoke with a hiss and pointed at her. Seconds later, he was sure he could see her camera aimed in his direction, and he drew his finger slowly across his throat.

***

With the time coming up to two in the afternoon, Gemma was called to Vickers' makeshift office in the traffic inspectors' room, where she brought him up to date.

"Cassons Dating Agency in Leeds are grumbling but willing to co-operate, sir. They're searching their databases for any trace of the four victims and any man common to them." Gemma rubbed the fatigue from her eyes. "I have to say I'm not hopeful. I've gone over the printouts from Angela Foster, and there is no link between the two women on their database… or, should I say, there is no man's name common to them, but considering Letty Hill used a false name it may be that the Sanford Dating Agency has the same man registered twice or more times, under different handles."

Vickers drew her daily report from his in-tray and studied it. "You were querying her false name, Collina?"

"Yes, sir. I don't know that there's anything in it, and wasn't there a famous football referee with the same name?"

Vickers grinned. "Yes there was, and there's no secret about it, Sergeant. It's Italian for hill."

"Ah. That explains that, then." Gemma shrugged. "Beyond that then, sir, it's all about what the team can turn up from wherever."

Vickers resumed his study of the report. "Murray has some interesting observations on this spoon business. Did you pass them on to Des Kibble?"

"Yes, sir. Haven't heard back from him yet."

Vickers picked up the phone and punched in a four digit extension number. "Kibble? My office, please, and ask Ingleton to come in with you and bring the photographs from Oakleigh Grove." He put the phone down.

"I don't think he likes me, sir," Gemma commented. "Your Des Kibble."

"He doesn't like anyone, Gemma. Not since—"

"His bit on the side went AWOL. I know, sir, you told me. But that doesn't excuse his rudeness, even with you."

"He's a good man. That's why we tolerate him." At the sound of a polite knock on the door, Vickers called, "In," and Kibble entered, followed by Ingleton who was carrying a large portfolio. "Ah, Des, Paul. Sergeant Craddock asked you to check on the cups and saucers left on the sink at Letty Hill's place. Did you?"

"Yes, sir," Kibble replied, "and frankly, Sergeant Craddock should get her facts right before she has the rest of us chasing wild geese."

Gemma glared daggers. "If you worked for me, you'd be on report for that remark."

"Well, let's both be grateful I don't work for you." Kibble nodded to Ingleton, who reached into the portfolio and drew out a photographic print, which he laid on the desk.

Gemma could see instantly it was an enlargement of the kitchen sink.

"Joe Murray said there was no spoon, sir," the photographer explained, "and that led him to speculate that the killer had made himself a brew after murdering Letty Hill. If you'd both looked carefully at the original, there is a spoon." He pointed at the far edge of the draining basket where the handle of a spoon could be made out between the grey plastic and the blue tiles of the window sill. "It can be seen on the original, too, if you look closely enough." He took out the original and placed it to one side of the enlargement.

"So it is. Hard to see, though," Vickers commented.

"Not if you pay close attention," Kibble replied with a withering glance at Gemma.

"Odd that Uncle Joe didn't see it," Gemma sniped. "He has an eagle's eye when it comes to such things."

Kibble made no effort to mask his cynicism. "Maybe he didn't want to see it."

"You can knock that off, too," Gemma warned. "This is an investigation, not a witch hunt."

"You can both knock it off," Vickers cut in before tempers

could flare. "What about dabs on the cup?"

"Partial on the handle, as Sergeant Craddock suggested, sir," Kibble reported, "but we'd logged it on Friday afternoon. It's an imprint, not a fingerprint, and my guess is it's a Marigold washing up glove." Kibble pointed to the chief inspector's folder. "It's all in my report."

"What about the rest of the house?" Vickers demanded.

"Prints everywhere, sir. Most are Letty Hill's, as you'd expect. Several sets I can positively identify as Joe Murray's, and some which are unidentified. Could be neighbours, could be tradesmen, could be anyone." Again Kibble pointed to the folder. "Again, it's all in the report."

"The tallboy," Gemma said, recalling her conversation with Joe. "Any dust patterns to indicate anything had been moved around?"

"Nothing," Kibble replied. "No dust on the tallboy. Letty was obviously a fastidious woman who cleaned regularly. No dust, no prints, nothing on any of the items." Scientific Support may have something on the polish she used, but I have nothing more for you." He turned soulless eyes on Gemma. "As far as I'm concerned, your uncle is the only suspect and I haven't found anything that will help you cross him off the list."

***

Dalmer handled the porcelain representation of *Pagliaccio* gingerly, turning it on its side, looking for the telltale mark of Meissen on the base.

"I'm always cautious when handling them," he chuckled. "Terrified of dropping them." He studied the crossed, blue marks underneath. "It appears genuine."

"It is," Sheila assured him. "Peter, my late husband, bought it for me on our twentieth wedding anniversary. He never said how much he paid for it, but I'm told it could be worth a lot of money now."

"They produce a limited number every year," Dalmer assured her. "As few as ten or twenty, and they retail at about two thousand pounds. This has been well cared for, and it could be worth considerably more." He put the piece back in Sheila's display cabinet. "I don't suppose it's for sale?"

Sheila shook her head. "I'm not in need of money, Stewart, and even if I were, I'd probably sell the house before that." She closed the cabinet. "There are other pieces you can make an offer for, if you wish." She pointed to a lower shelf and two separate pieces; a cat and a dog, both sitting. "Certified Delft. We bought them on a trip to Amsterdam. I think they cost about fifty pounds for the pair."

"I like Delft," Dalmer agreed, "and I'd be happy to pay you, say thirty for the pair, but Meissen… Ah, that is something really special."

Sheila smiled good-naturedly. "I'm sorry. I'll take your offer on the Delft, but not the Meissen."

Dalmer took out his wallet and retrieved three ten-pound notes, which he handed over. Sheila went back into the cabinet and removed the two items. Taking them from her, he reached into his briefcase and came out with two, small, flattened boxes. While Sheila went to the kitchen to make tea, he made the boxes up, packed in a lower layer of tissue, placed the ornaments in, then added an upper layer of tissue before putting on the lids. Marking them and taping the lids in place, he put them back in his briefcase, closed and locked it, and put it carefully on the carpet alongside one of the chairs at Sheila's walnut dining table.

Gazing through the leaded windows at the quiet, suburban street outside, he reminded himself that they were just a few streets from Letty Hill's place, and Sheila's home was the same kind of bungalow.

Like others who had visited the house, Dalmer could not help the feeling that it was more of a shrine than a home; a memorial dedicated to Sheila's late husband, Inspector Peter Riley. Aside from the few items of china, the display cabinet, and two others spread around the room, were filled with photographs of her and her husband, and many of Peter alone, augmented by photographs of their two children, Peter Jnr, and Aaron.

Sheila returned with the tea tray, placed it on the table and invited Dalmer to help himself.

"I know I'm speaking to a police widow," Dalmer said as he poured tea into a rose china cup, "but you are well protected against burglary, aren't you Sheila?"

"I have the latest alarms fitted, double deadlocks on all doors and windows and, of course, I never leave windows open when I'm not in. And there are only three keys to the house. I have one, a second is in the kitchen drawer and Brenda Jump has the third." As he put the teapot down, Sheila picked it up and poured for herself. "Joe harasses us about safety all the time." She smiled fondly. "I know he's a grumpy old so-and-so, but deep down, he really does care. Anyway, because we're the best of friends and we both live alone, I gave Brenda a key to my house and I have one for hers. If either of us is ever taken ill, the other can always get in to help." The smile faded, replaced with a frown. "Poor Joe. I do wish the police would sort this business out. It's so depressing for him."

"They haven't officially cleared him yet?"

Gently stirring milk into her tea, Sheila shook her head. "The investigation is ongoing. I don't for one minute, think they really suspect him, but he was one of the last people to see poor Letty, so he remains a suspect until they can find something that clears him." She brightened up. "Enough about Joe Murray. Tell me about you and your antiques business."

"Not a business as such. More of a hobby, really. I buy and sell occasional items; china, silverware, jewellery. I don't have premises and I work mostly online, but when it's someone in the local area, like you, I enjoy visiting and looking over the pieces." He smiled broadly. "Like your *Pagliaccio*."

Sheila wagged a mock-disapproving finger at him. "I told you. Not for sale."

Sipping his tea, he took out his wallet again. "Let me leave you my card, just in case you change your mind." He handed over the plain white card.

Sheila studied it a moment. "You don't even put your name on it? Nothing but your initials and a phone number. And even that's a mobile."

He nodded and drank more tea. "And I never answer it. Callers have to leave a message and a number and I get back to them." He took in her look of suspicion and laughed. "There's nothing sinister in it, Sheila. Antique dealing is a strange business. Most traders are honest, but there are plenty of rogues about. Morton Norris is one. I don't say he deliberately tries to con people, but he does tell some tall stories when he's selling. He tried to pass off a china Shepherd Boy from Stoke on Trent as Meissen. I saw through it right away. By keeping my name off the card and giving only a mobile number, which I never answer, and where the caller has to leave a message, I avoid most of the conmen."

Sheila tucked the card in her purse. "How very sensible."

Chapter Nine

Joe had spent so many years crawling out of bed before five in the morning that even without the alarm set his body clock woke him at the same hour.

Rolling out of bed, he parted the blinds a couple of inches and looked out on a quiet, frosty Doncaster Road. It would be another hour before the level of traffic picked up, and even then it would be mainly lorries making for the motorway.

Across the dual carriageway, outside Broadbent's, sat Rosemary Ecclesfield's Peugeot, its windows covered in either condensation or, more likely, ice. Joe's lip curled. After the confrontation the previous day, the stupid woman had driven away about three o'clock, only to return just before seven, and judging from her windscreen, she must have been parked there all night. Mick Chadwick had called him at ten to say that she had been in the Miner's Arms for an hour, asking after him. But Joe had not moved from his flat all night, other than to visit Patel's next door at six, where he collected a pack of tobacco and a copy of the *Sanford Gazette*.

To his relief, the newspaper did not mention him, although there was some coverage of the police investigation into Letty's death. Not that there was much to report, other than the inquiry had widened to take in businesses in Leeds and Wakefield.

With a gaping yawn, dismissing thoughts of Rosemary Ecclesfield, Joe let the blinds fall shut, moved to the bathroom, showered and shaved, and by five-fifteen, he was sat before his netbook, chewing through a bowl of cereal while he read over his notes on the case so far.

He had always been meticulous in making notes. It often helped him spot the tiny inconsistencies which led him to successful outcomes. In this case, there was so little that he could learn nothing from them. They could not point him at a suspect because he *was* the suspect. Neither could the notes point him to inconsistencies in stories because there were no accounts other than his and the police's. He did, however, find reminders to speak with Gemma on the missing spoon and her inquiries with Cassons in Leeds.

He would be the first to admit that he was no expert on serial killers, but the whole case was baffling. What was this business with laying the bodies on the bed, pushing up their skirts to expose their underwear? Valentine's Night, too, indicated some kind of sexual motivation, and yet there had never been any trace of molestation in any of the killings. What was this man playing at?

At five thirty, he made his way downstairs and into the café. It was all very well for Sheila and Brenda to suggest taking a few days off, but neither of them had volunteered to show up early, and Cheryl could never get in before seven because she had to leave young Danny with her mother, who would not be up before then. So, even though he was supposed to be taking time off, he still had to open up, let Lee in, and get breakfast on the move before the dray men began to turn up.

"Morning, Uncle Joe," Lee chirped as he breezed in.

"Kettle's boiling up, Lee. Make us both a brew, will you?"

"Roger, cobbler."

Joe tutted. His brother, Arthur, Lee's father, had much to answer for by emigrating to Australia.

He scowled across the road at the dormant Peugeot. "Freeze, you silly mare. You'll get nothing on me."

At half past six, by which time Joe had served the first few passing truckers, Amir Patel, the fifteen-year-old son of the minimarket proprietor next door, dropped the *Daily Express* in.

"Hey up, Uncle Joe, is it right you've murdered that woman from t'other side of town?" For all that the boy had roots in Pakistan, his accent was pure Yorkshire, and like many of the local children, they had grown up calling him Uncle Joe.

"Just deliver the papers, Amir. You don't have to believe everything you read in them."

"I'm glad about that. Me dad says the cops have got it wrong again. Just like when they did you for dumping all that chip fat in the back lane, when it weren't you."

Feeling slightly encouraged, Joe settled behind the counter and studied the crossword. He considered the Patels and Dennis Walmsley who ran the DIY shop at the end of the parade, to be more than simply fellow traders. They were genuine neighbours of the old fashioned kind. The Lazy Luncheonette had stood there under one guise or another since the end of World War Two, Dennis and his wife had opened up in the late eighties, using his redundancy payoff from the mines, and the Patels had opened up a few years later.

Sheila, Brenda and Cheryl all arrived at a few minutes to seven, all shivering from the icy blasts blowing along the road.

"You're not the only ones feeling the chill," Joe said, nodding through the windows and across the road to the static Peugeot.

Closing the door, Brenda peered through the glass. "How long has she been there?"

"All night, I think," Joe replied, settling back at table five with his crossword.

"She must be freezing," Sheila commented. Passing through to the kitchen she hung up her coat and put on her tabard. "Right, Joe, you can go whenever you like. Get your problems sorted."

"I'm in no hurry."

"Yes you are," Brenda said. "The dray men will be here in

ten minutes, and we need every seat we can get. Clear off and be a man of leisure for a day or two."

Fastening her tabard, pinning up her cap, Sheila suggested, "Why not take that reporter a cup of tea, Joe?"

His laugh dripped cynicism. "What? Laced with cyanide or arsenic. Tell you what, just to be sure, let's put both in. The trouble she's caused people with her poisoned pen, no judge would ever convict me."

Sheila disappeared into the kitchen. "I'm thinking community relations, Joe," she called back.

"So was I when I thought of poisoning her."

Sheila returned with tea in a polystyrene takeaway cup. She placed it in front of Joe, and then put two sachets of sugar and a plastic spoon alongside it.

Joe glowered up. "I didn't realise you meant it."

"I did. Think common sense, Joe. She hates you right now because you chased her out yesterday, but if you go over there with a cup of hot tea as a peace offering, she may be prepared to listen to your side of the story."

"Makes sense to me," Brenda commented, making the rounds of the tables to check on the condiments.

"Tell me you're just taking the mickey," Joe pleaded.

Sheila pressed her finger on the lid of the cup and pushed it to him. "Go, Joe. You know you have to."

Joe stared through the windows, across to the car growing more visible in the dawn. He did not want to leave the warm sanctity of his café, he did not want to build bridges with this woman who had stalked him so assiduously. He really did feel like poisoning her. But Sheila was rarely wrong, and there was something so insistent about her actions that told him it was the right thing to do.

Grumbling, he folded his newspaper away, picked up the cup, sugar and spoon, and hurried out of the café as the first dray lorry pulled into the back lane.

Wearing only his whites and a thin T-Shirt, the shock of

cold hit him like a sledgehammer, the moment he left the café, and with the early traffic picking up, getting across Doncaster Road was a life and death proposition. It would be easier in an hour when the daily jam slowed traffic to a crawl, but at seven fifteen, drivers came on too fast towards the double set of lights, and Joe felt it took a good minute or more to get across, by which time he was shivering.

"If I'm this cold, how bad is she," he grumbled while making his way into the industrial estate and up the slight rise to her parked car. "Not that I really care."

All the windows were covered in a layer of frost and ice. Joe rapped on the driver's door and got no response.

"Come on, lady. You're pushing charity too far."

He rapped on the glass this time, and still there was no response.

Was she actually in the car?

It was a question which should have occurred to him when he first looked out of his bedroom window. And now that he asked it, several reasons why she would not be there sprang to mind, not least of which was the cold. The car could have broken down. She could have left it there just to spite and intimidate him. She could have been drunk in the Miner's Arms last night, and taken a taxi home instead.

Warming the palm of his hand on the plastic cup, Joe rubbed at the frost. He felt as if his hand was going to freeze to the glass, but he managed to cut a rough swathe through the icy coating; enough to let him see her sat behind the wheel.

The interior of the glass was frozen too, so all he could make out was a blurred shape. He rubbed once more at the window, called out, "Hey, sleepy head, I brought you a hot drink," and then, when she still did not respond, he leaned closer.

Her mouth was open, tongue lolling grotesquely out. Her eyes were open, staring, not seeing. A thin cord was buried deep in the soft flesh around her neck.

It was like an electric shock. Joe leapt back, the plastic cup spilling from his hand, hot tea splashing on the pavement and melting the ice as it spread. Joe's heart pounded. He stared frantically around, seeking help which was not there. He patted his pockets. His mobile, the number most people rang when they wanted to place an order, was in the café.

Looking back at the Lazy Luncheonette, he ran for it.

***

"For the last time, Vickers, I found her like that. I did not kill her."

Because Joe knew so many of the Sanford police, Vickers had elected to take his statement, and he did so in the privacy of Joe's apartment, where they could not be interrupted by café staff or customers. And after Joe had read and signed the statement, Vickers began to throw the inevitable questions.

"You don't deny chasing her out of the café?" the chief inspector demanded and Joe shook his head. "You don't deny ringing the editor of the *Sanford Gazette*?" Again Joe shook his head. "Issuing threats?"

"The only threat I made against Lofthouse was to withdraw the Sanford 3rd Age Club's advertising."

Vickers put down his pen and stared through the windows. Joe followed suit. Across Doncaster Road, police vehicles and officers swarmed around the white tent which had been erected to conceal the dead woman's car. Mechanics, apprentices and office staff from Broadbent's regarded it as a form of entertainment and could regularly be seen taking a smoke break with eyes on the police and forensic activity. Drivers in the Doncaster Road jam also regarded the events as a spectator sport, and it seemed to Joe that the traffic moved even slower than usual. Vickers had arrived before eight o'clock, Rosemary's body had been removed by half past eight, carried away in a body bag on a shrouded trolley, and after speaking with his SOCOs, learning that Joe had raised the alarm, the chief inspector had made his way to the Lazy Luncheonette.

That was at nine. Gemma, Joe was told, had been sent to the *Sanford Gazette* to see what they had to say, and with the time coming up to ten, Vickers was still here, badgering, trying to secure a confession, while Joe resisted.

And through it all, the angry confusion ringing through Joe's head increased. Someone was trying to make him a patsy. Why? Was it personal? Was it simply to deflect the police from the truth. And who was it?

When he thought about it, everything came down to one question, which had been bouncing round his head. Vickers put it into words. "What did Rosemary Ecclesfield and Letitia Hill have in common?"

Joe already knew the answer. "Me."

The chief inspector shrugged. "There you go."

Joe rolled a cigarette, and lit it. Drawing in the smoke, letting it out with a long, calming hiss, he fastened Vickers' gaze with his own. "Do you think I'm a complete fool?"

The chief inspector did not answer immediately. He picked up his pen, a Schaeffer finished in matt silver, and toyed with it. It seemed as if he were considering the question, or, more likely, formulating his answer.

"No," he said eventually. "I don't like you. We both know that, but personal feelings aside, I think you're rude, but clever and observant. In short, I think you're a smartarse, but unlike most such people, you don't just spout. You get to the right answers." He leaned forward, and jammed a pointed finger into the tabletop. "But this is different, Murray. Two women are dead. You are known to be amongst the last people Letitia Hill saw. The simple fact that I can find little evidence to say you killed her is meaningless. You know how to spot evidence, so you also know how to conceal it. And as of this moment, I have no evidence at all concerning Rosemary Ecclesfield." He gestured through the window. "I'm still waiting for it. What I do know is that you had a blazing row with her yesterday. Your staff confirmed it, you've admitted it. That's my starting point. It is enough for me to suspect that you had something to do with her death."

"Finished?" Joe waited for Vickers to nod. "Right, now let me tell you why I asked. Ever since you named me last Friday, that silly bitch has been sat on my doorstep taking pictures of me. I noticed her. She disappeared about three-ish yesterday afternoon. If I was going to shine her on, don't you think I'd have followed her and done it somewhere other than across the road from my home?"

Vickers opened his mouth to speak, Joe carried on.

"I'll tell you something else, as well. You don't have one jot of evidence against me. You just said so. You say it's because I'm being careful, I say it's because I had nothing to do with either killing. And when you come round to realising the truth, it's going to cost you a bloody fortune in compensation. I will sue your arse for every lost penny in trade, the damage to my good name, and the stress you've put me under. Now if you wanna make yourself really useful, Vickers, stop trying to pin the Valentine Strangler's work on me, get out there and find him."

Vickers was unfazed by the rebuke. "You had a blazing argument with her yesterday. So why did you feel you had to take her a cup of tea this morning? Simply charity or were you looking for an excuse to cross the road and 'discover' her body?" the chief inspector described speech marks in the air as he stressed the word 'discover'.

"If you listened to my staff, you'd know," Joe retorted. "It wasn't my idea, it was Sheila's. I said at the time, I'd have laced the tea with poison, but even if I had, it wouldn't matter. She was already dead."

Vickers did not reply. He fumed for a long time, and he was about to collect his belongings and leave, when there was a knock at the door. Without waiting for an answer, Gemma entered, her features grim.

"Morning, sir, morning Uncle Joe."

"Problems?" Joe asked.

"I wouldn't say problems exactly." She put her briefcase down on the settee, perched next to it, opened it, and took out sheets of printed A4 which she passed to Vickers. "The copy Rosemary filed with Ian Lofthouse at half past five yesterday afternoon. She also had a range of pictures of you, Joe, Angela Foster, Mort Norris and George Robson." She laid the photographs on the table for Joe to study.

There were a number of him; leaving the Lazy Luncheonette, walking round the market, going into the supermarket with Gemma, going into the Sanford Dating Agency with Gemma. There were also deliberately posed photographs of Mort Norris, presumably taken while he and Gemma were talking to Angie Foster, and a long range shot of Joe talking to both George Robson and Vinny Gillespie. Finally, there was another deliberate pose, taken later in the afternoon in Joe's opinion, of Angela Foster outside her office.

Disregarding the pictures, Joe glanced first at the printed sheets, then at Gemma. "Bad news?"

Gemma shushed him while Vickers read.

It did not take long. And when he looked up, Vickers' eyes gleamed with triumph. "No evidence, Murray? Good bit of circumstantial here. Read it."

Joe took the sheets and read through them.

Neatly word-processed in double line spacing, they made his blood run first cold, then hot.

IS THIS THE VALENTINE STRANGLER? The headline blazed in capital letters.

Joe Murray is well-known throughout Sanford as the rude and irritable proprietor of the Lazy Luncheonette truck stop on Doncaster Road. But on Friday, West Yorkshire police arrested Murray in connection with the Valentine Strangler killings. He was later released without charge, and yet the police know that MURRAY WAS ONE OF THE LAST PEOPLE TO SEE LETITIA HILL ALIVE.

This reporter followed up the case and learned that Murray, along with Detective Sergeant Gemma Craddock of Sanford CID, spoke to Angela Foster, proprietor of the Sanford Dating Agency of which Mrs Hill was a member under her real name of Letitia Collina. He was also seen to be talking with market trader, Morton Norris, a second hand goods dealer who was also one of Letitia's friends. I followed him to Sanford Memorial park where he spoke with landscaping supervisor, George Robson, one of Letitia's former lovers. Shortly after, Sanford police allowed Murray to drive away without penalty despite the fact that Murray was parked on double yellow lines.

Further inquiry has revealed that Detective Sergeant Craddock is MURRAY'S NIECE.

In an effort to get to the bottom of this near-Masonic conspiracy, I visited the Lazy Luncheonette on Monday afternoon where I confronted Murray. I was chased from the café by a furious Joe Murray threatening me with a kitchen implement.

It's time to ask some serious questions about Joe Murray's close links with the police. If he is guilty, why has he been released? Why does he go unpunished for minor infringements of the law? How much influence does he have at Gale Street? Why is his niece permitted to work on the investigation? What right does Murray have to question others who have close links to the victim, and what right does he have to threaten a reporter, seeking only the facts, with physical violence?

The time has come to protect the public from this monster.

Joe snatched up his mobile and dialled the *Gazette*.

"Now, Murray—"

Joe cut Vickers off and barked into the phone. "It's Joe Murray. Gimme Ian Lofthouse, now before my lawyers start beating down his door."

"You can't do this, Uncle Joe," Gemma warned him.

"No? Watch me." A click at the other end told Joe he was through. "Lofthouse? It's Joe Murray. I've just read this crap Gemma brought back from your place. When were you going to tell me about it?"

"Well, I wasn't," Lofthouse replied. "Joe, Rosemary was asking some serious questions."

"She was producing a load of old tripe, and you know it. There are more lies in these few pages than your last tax return."

"Lies? What lies?"

"Let's start with my arrest," Joe insisted. "I was not arrested." He glanced across at Vickers' thunderous features. "I may be. Any time now, but last Friday I went to the police station of my own free will and gave them a statement. Let's move on to Angela Foster and the Sanford Dating Agency. I did not browbeat her into anything. My niece asked a few questions, and that's it. Next, Mort Norris was never a friend of Letty's, and George Robson was not one of Letty's lovers, and finally, Collina was not Letty's real name."

"But you did chase her from your place with a kitchen implement?" Lofthouse asked.

"It was a teapot, you idiot. What do you think I'd do with it? Pour hot tea all over her hair?"

"And you do have links with the law."

"I help them occasionally and if Vinny Gillespie let me off with a ticket, it was down to negotiation, not funny handshakes."

The editor harrumphed. "Yes, well, you needn't worry, Joe. At the insistence of the police, we won't be running the story."

"Then you should thank the cops, because if you did, you'd be hearing from my solicitor. Now do us all a favour, Ian, and get off my back." Joe killed the connection and glowered at the chief inspector. "Well?"

Vickers held his thumb and forefinger a few millimetres apart. "You are this close to being arrested, Murray."

"Then get on with it," Joe challenged. "Because the moment you do, my lawyers will be all over you like a cheap suit, too."

Refusing to rise to the bait, Vickers rounded on Gemma. "As of this moment, Sergeant, you are off the case."

"Sir—"

"Don't take it out on her," Joe interrupted.

"I'm not," Vickers insisted. "The investigation is already compromised and I won't have it dragged any further down into the mud.

"I think it might be more to the point, sir, if we found out who told Rosemary Ecclesfield that Joe is my uncle. It's not common knowledge, other than in the family and at the station."

"And I don't see what difference that makes," Vickers retorted.

"Angela Foster is who told her," Joe replied. "Remember, you let it slip when we were speaking to her."

Gemma blushed. "I'm sorry."

"Angela Foster is also the one who gave Ecclesfield the bottom line on Mort Norris and George Robson."

"You can't know that," Vickers argued.

Joe nodded. "You're right, but it's reasonable to assume it. When we spoke to her, she was at pains to point out that she only makes pennies on the dating agency. She'd do anything to hype the name a little, and that's just what she has done. She knows Mort Norris – or, at least, Mort knows her – and as for George… well, he's so busy with the women of this town, that it wouldn't surprise me to learn he's been a member of the Sanford Dating Agency at some time or another."

"And Gillespie letting you off with a parking ticket?" Vickers demanded. "I suppose Angela Foster told Ecclesfield about that, too, did she?"

"No," Joe replied. "Rosemary saw it happen. She was parked a little further up the road… on double yellow lines.

And she didn't get a ticket, either."

There was another knock on the door. Vickers barked a command and Des Kibble entered, still clad in his white, forensic coveralls. Vickers raised eyebrows at him.

"Very little, sir. No prints other than Rosemary Ecclesfield's anywhere on the car, other than his on the drivers' window." Kibble jerked a thumb at Joe.

"Where I rubbed the frost off," Joe said before Vickers could take any satisfaction from the announcement.

Kibble nodded confirmation, and Vickers asked, "Doc have anything to say?"

"She was strangled from behind," Kibble said. "Whoever did it was sat in the rear seat."

The chief inspector swung his attention on Joe. "You said you'd seen her out there all night? Did you see anyone else in the vicinity?"

"No."

"Then she must have invited the killer into the car."

Joe shook his head. "Not necessarily. Think about this, Vickers. I had a call from Mick Chadwick at the Miner's Arms last night. Rosemary Ecclesfield had been in there asking about me. It's half a mile up the road. I never saw her car move, so she must have walked it. Mick rang me at ten. Suppose, while she was gone, someone got into her car and lay low on the back seat?"

"You'd have seen him," Vickers objected.

Joe fumed. "I wasn't watching her every minute of the night, for God's sake. And from across the road it wouldn't be too difficult for anyone to work out whether I was at the window. They would have seen me."

Vickers rounded on Kibble. "And there are no other traces in the car?"

"Not from my point of view, sir. I dunno if Scientific Support will turn up anything. They're waiting for the wrecker to come and take the car away."

Vickers stood, tucked Joe's signed statement and the press sheets into his briefcase and locked it up. "I don't have enough evidence to arrest you, Murray, so for the time being, you're in the clear. But I may be back. Don't go anywhere without letting me know. Sergeant Craddock, I repeat, you are now officially off this investigation. I'll call a press conference for this afternoon and see if I can't salvage some credibility." He glared down at Joe. "And if Scientific Support find one trace of you, even a drop of cigarette ash, I'll be back mob handed."

Chapter Ten

With Vickers gone, Gemma smiled wanly at her uncle. "I'm sorry."

He snorted softly. "Yeah. Me too. Vickers is determined to see me swing for this."

Gemma moved to the table and joined him. "That's not strictly true. You had an argument with her yesterday; you were heard to threaten her... I know, I know," she pressed on before he could interrupt. "It was only temper talking, but just the same, if Vickers didn't follow it up, he wouldn't be doing his job."

"He's enjoying his job," Joe pointed out.

"That may well be, but he has to follow it up. I don't believe he seriously suspects you. He wouldn't have ordered me to let you see those photographs last Friday if he did. As for me..." She sighed. "I should never have been on the investigation in the first place."

"It won't affect your job, or your, er, promotion prospects?"

Gemma laughed cynically. "Hmph. What promotion prospects? I have to leave Sanford if I want to get on. No, no, it won't affect my job. It might affect his, or it would have done if he hadn't dropped me from the team. But he's right, Uncle Joe. I'm your niece. I'm too close to it all." She grinned slyly. "That doesn't mean to say I can't find out what's going on, though."

Joe laughed for the first time in what seemed like days. "You're a good girl, Gemma, I should have married your mum instead of her sister, then you'd have been my little girl." He checked the time and collected his tobacco tin. "Come on. The morning rush will be over. Let's go downstairs and get a brew."

Joe was only half right. The morning rush of lorry drivers was over, and usually the follow-on of shoppers from Sanford Retail Park would be done, too, but when they passed through the kitchen, they found the café as crowded as ever, most of the customers watching events over the road where Rosemary Ecclesfield's car was being cranked onto a flatbed salvage truck.

"Tell you what, Joe," Brenda said, "a murder across the road isn't half good for business. I've never seen it so busy."

"Nowhere to sit," Gemma said. "I'd better get back to the station, Uncle Joe. I'll catch you all later."

"Yeah, sure, Gemma. Let me know if you hear anything."

With her gone, Joe found himself superfluous to requirements.

"Best thing you can do is clear off, Joe," Brenda suggested. "You're just getting under everyone's feet here."

"Maybe you're right. Think I'll have a ride into town."

"And do what?" Sheila asked.

"Talk to Mort Norris… again." Joe threw on his coat and made for the back door.

In direct contrast to his journey to Gale Street on Friday, Joe was well-rehearsed by the time he parked in the multi storey car park, and made his way through the cold, near-empty streets of Sanford to the market, where he found Mort in the same mufti as he had been the previous day.

"You're in trouble again, I believe, Joe."

"Word spreads quickly."

Mort agreed. "Gets round this town faster than the flu, mate. I knew this reporter bird was dead ten minutes after I got here this morning."

"Yep, and you know something, Mort. Through all this talk, one name keeps cropping up. Yours."

Mort looked convincingly shocked. "Mine? Come on, Joe I

didn't kill neither of 'em?"

"No, but you've been telling tales outta school, haven't you?"

"I—"

"You spoke to that reporter yesterday, didn't you? No point flannelling, Mort. I know you did."

Mort shoulders sagged. "Yeah, I talked to her."

"And dropped me right in it."

"It wasn't like that, Joe. Come on, pal, I'm like you. A businessman. The way things are, I need all the help I can get, and she promised to identify me as what I am."

"A big mouth?"

"A market trader. Jeez, Joe, it amounts to free advertising. She just wanted to know about you and Letty Hill, so I told her."

"And dropped me and George in it. She identified him in her piece."

Mort frowned. "I ain't seen anything in the *Gazette*."

"Because the police pulled it. She told a pack of lies about me, and George, and she got them from you. George never scored with Letty."

"He coulda lied to you," Mort said hopefully.

"Since when did George keep his conquests secret?" Joe challenged. "Luckily for you, like I said, the law got the paper to pull the story, but all the bull you fed her is what got her killed. She was so obsessed with pinning it all on me, that she turned herself into a sitting duck. You wanna think about that before you go opening your mouth next time, Mort."

***

When she stepped back into the station, Gemma found it a hive of activity, Vickers readying to leave with a small team of detectives.

"What's going on?" she asked.

"We're recovering from your errors, Sergeant," Vickers snapped. "If you'd done your job right, we could have been there a year or maybe two years ago."

Gemma suppressed her immediate anger. "I don't know what you mean, sir."

Vickers led her across to his desk and a small stack of reports. "Lists of victims' personal effects. Fiona Temple: a small white card. Thelma Warburton: plain white business card, printed SDA. Bridget Ackroyd: business card, no name. Letitia Hill: Sanford Dating Agency business card." He gestured at Kibble. "When Des checked them, they were all the same type of card. Plain, white, printed with the letters SDA. The Sanford Dating Agency. Four different descriptions of the same item. No wonder we couldn't find a link."

"We may have logged the card the first time of asking, sir, but you took over the investigation after Thelma Warburton's murder, and it was your people who didn't do their jobs right."

Vickers brushed off her objection. "Be that as it may, Angela Foster lied to you yesterday. All four women were members of her dating agency, and there was one name you didn't check on."

"Whose?"

"Joe bloody Murray."

"He's not a member," Gemma replied. "He can't be. He asked Foster yesterday and she wouldn't have him."

"You mean he's not a member under his real name, but if Letty Hill could join under an Italian pseudonym what price Joe Murray could, too? And he asked her yesterday to throw you off the scent, knowing damn well she'd refuse. We're going over there now and we're gonna tear that database to pieces until we find him."

Gemma fixed his gaze. "With all due respect, sir, I believe you're wrong about Joe. You're so obsessed with him that it's blinding you to other possibilities."

"And with the same respect, Sergeant, don't tell me how to

do my job, or you'll find yourself working for the nearest security firm." Vickers stormed from the office.

Gemma stared after his back, then, making up her mind, walked out of the station into the cold afternoon. Climbing into her car, she fired the engine, took out her mobile and rang Joe.

"Yeah, Gemma, what can I do you for?"

"Where are you?"

"Sanford. I was just gonna visit Angela Foster, but she isn't in."

"Get back in your car, go back to the Lazy Luncheonette and I'll meet you there in fifteen minutes."

"What? But—"

"Just do it, Uncle Joe. Vickers is out to make an arrest and you're the target. I need to speak to you if we're to head him off."

***

On the other side of Doncaster Road, aside from a few Scientific Support officers, there was nothing left of the murder scene and the Lazy Luncheonette's trade had settled to normal levels, but when they met, the lunchtime rush was in full swing. Joe managed to find them seats in the window, where his niece outlined the situation to him.

"He's barking up the wrong tree, Gemma," Joe assured her. "Let him go through the database. He won't find me on it. All he's doing is wasting his time."

Gemma was not so certain. "He's determined to get you, Joe, and I wouldn't put it past him to find something, anything that will help him pin you down."

"What?" Joe was open-mouthed. "If he's fabricating evidence—"

"That's not what I meant," Gemma interrupted. "He's a good copper; an honest copper. He wouldn't invent anything, but if he finds anyone who looks remotely like you, he'll haul you in." She tutted and cradled a beaker of tea in her palms. "If we'd logged this business card thing properly, we wouldn't be in this position. We'd have been onto the dating agency a year, maybe two years ago. We may even have had the killer."

Joe shrugged. "No point worrying about might have beens, but thinking about it, if you're right about Vickers, he could get something. I have a Sanford Dating Agency card."

Gemma's eyebrows rose and a look of suspicion slowly spread across her face. "You do?"

"Yes. I took one the other day… yesterday, when we were talking to Angela Foster."

Relief replaced the doubt. "Oh. Right. Well, at least I can account for that. Uncle Joe, you're sure you've never used this agency."

"I've never used any agency, chicken. The few dates I've had since your Aunt Alison left have been, er, *engineered*, let's say, in the normal way. I asked women out, or in the case of Letty Hill, Brenda asked her out for me." Joe stared moodily through the window at two Scientific Support officers making a fingertip search of the pavements. "He's gotta be on the right, track, though, Gemma. There must be some connection between the four women."

"And dating agencies are the only lead we have. Slim, but we've nothing else."

They fell silent for a moment, watching events outside.

"Nothing else happened?" Joe asked.

"Hmm? What? Oh. No… well, Tim Hill turned up."

Joe frowned. "Tim Hill? Oh, Letty's son?"

"Yes. Flew in from Brussels first thing. He's at her bungalow now. He's a bit to get through. Furniture and stuff to get rid of, house to put on the market. You know the script."

"Yeah. Poor sod. Must be terrible…"

He trailed off at the sound of a sudden furore from the

kitchen, which silenced everyone, including the diners.

"I don't give a damn who you are or what you want," he heard Brenda shout. "You can't come through here. It's a hygiene area. Go round the front."

Muffled, male voices bit back.

"Lee, throw 'em out," Brenda snapped.

Joe got to his feet and hurried to the kitchen door, where he found Brenda and Lee confronting Chief Inspector Vickers and two CID officers.

"What's going on?" Joe demanded.

Vickers pointed a shaking finger at him. "You're under arrest, Murray."

"Am I? Well Brenda is right. This is a hygiene area, and you'll be getting a bill for the cleaning and any food we have to waste. Now bugger off and get some people to find your brain. I'm sure they'll figure out where you've left it."

Gemma arrived behind him. "What's going on, sir?"

The chief inspector glared. "I thought I might find you here. As of this moment, Sergeant, you are suspended from duty pending an internal inquiry." Drawing in his breath, he concentrated on Joe. When he spoke, his voice was calm, mechanical. "Joseph Murray, I am arresting you on suspicion of murder. You do not have to say anything, but it may harm your defence if you fail to mention when questioned something which you intend to rely on in court. Anything you say may be given in evidence."

"Anything I say? How about, Vickers, you're a damned idiot." Joe signalled to Sheila at the counter, and passed his keys to her. "When they need to search my apartment, Sheila, let them in and make sure they don't steal anything." He glowered at Vickers. "Or plant anything."

***

Joe declined legal advice. "I don't need some high-priced

legal eagle to tie you in knots, Vickers," he said.

In the presence of the chief inspector and a bulky detective constable, the interview room felt even more cramped than when he had faced Vickers and Gemma.

Vickers began the interrogation while the DC took notes. "We're questioning you on the four killings which have become known as the work of the Sanford Valentine Strangler. In the past two hours, certain facts have come to light which indicate a connection between the four victims and you. First, let me ask you, have you ever been a member of the Sanford Dating Agency?"

"No. Never."

"Not under your own or any other name."

"Not under any name."

"In that case, Murray, how do you explain your address and a photograph of you appearing in the Sanford Dating Agency database?"

"I can't," Joe replied. "Someone else must have registered me without my knowledge."

Vickers harrumphed. "How would that be possible?"

"The way Angela Foster works, anything is possible. Show me this entry."

Vickers reached to the floor and from a folder took a sheet of A4. He turned it to face Joe.

The name on the entry was Murray Josephson, but the address was Doncaster Road, Sanford, and the picture was undoubtedly him, even though his eyes were shaded by the peak of his flat cap.

"Very interesting," Joe said and pushed the sheet back, "but it's nothing to do with me."

"You insist someone else has set this up?"

"I do, and for very good reasons."

"And those are?"

Joe pointed to the sheet, now the wrong way up. "My address is not Doncaster Road, but Britannia Parade."

"A simple enough ruse," Vickers observed. "One which you could have thought of."

"True, but the cap is a different matter, isn't it?"

The chief inspector frowned and the DC looked up, puzzled.

"The cap?" Vickers asked.

"The cap." Joe pointed to the printed sheet. "You see, Vickers, according to the details on that paper, I joined the Sanford Dating Agency four years ago, but the cap in that photograph is a dark blue with a tartan pattern. I only bought it last year, and if you need any proof of that, ask my girls, Sheila and Brenda. They were with me when I bought it. Cost me twelve pounds in Marks and Spencer's, Scarborough."

Vickers was momentarily flummoxed. He went into whispered conversation with his subordinate. A moment later, he turned back to Joe.

"You could have updated your photograph last year for all we know."

"Again, true," Joe replied, "but if you interrogated the database properly, you'd soon learn that, wouldn't you?"

Vickers frowned. "What?"

Joe sighed. "I thought you were supposed to be a professional, Vickers? At least that's what my niece told me. If you hack the database on Angela Foster's system, it'll tell you what updates have been made to my alleged account, and when they were made. If you then take my computers from home, and check them, you'll learn that I've been nowhere near that site, ever."

"You could have used an internet café."

Joe smiled. "With my aversion to spending money? Get real, Vickers. I told you I didn't need a lawyer to tie you in knots."

***

Feeling lower than at any time she could ever recall, Gemma stepped into the Sanford Dating Agency to find Des Kibble and Paul Ingleton at the rear of the room working on their laptops. She guessed they were downloading different sectors of the agency's database.

Kibble greeted her arrival with a barrage of complaints. "According to our information, you're suspended," he shouted.

"And for all you know I might be looking for a date," Gemma snapped. "Just shut up and get on with your work." She turned to Angela Foster. "I'm sorry to bother you, Mrs Foster, but this business is driving a lot of people round the bend."

As Angela was about to reply, Kibble left his laptop and marched over to the counter. "Either get out or I'll phone the chief."

Ingleton was right behind him. "Steady on, Des."

"She has no business asking questions here."

The photographer made another effort to soothe him. "Just cool it, buddy. No need to get excited?"

Gemma glared. "Listen to your partner, Kibble. Ring who you like, but don't forget my rank. Speak to me like that again and I really will give you a reason to hate women."

Kibble backed off, moved back to his computer, and picked up his mobile. Gemma could hear him muttering into it.

Ingleton smiled ingratiatingly at her. "Sorry about that, Sarge, but he does have a point. You really shouldn't be here."

"I know, but I'm trying to stop your chief inspector from leading the Sanford police up the wrong tree." She turned to Angela. "Mrs Foster, how is it possible for Uncle Joe's details to appear on your computer, and how is it possible for these women to be in possession of your business card yet not appear on your system?"

"Well, as I said yesterday, the business card isn't difficult to get hold of, and I'm sorry, but Mr Murray could have used a false name. It was definitely him, though. I recognised him the moment Chief Inspector Vickers showed me the photograph."

"Uncle Joe insists he only picked up your card yesterday. Did you give it to him?"

Angela appeared almost insulted by the question. "I most certainly did not. I made it clear that he would be unwelcome as a member."

"Then how did he get it?"

Angie pointed along the counter at her display of leaflets. "He took one of those. Each leaflet has a business card inside. Leaflets tend to get thrown in the dustbin, Sergeant, but most people will usually keep a business card."

Gemma took a leaflet and opened it out. Inside were images of young men and women holding hands, holidaying, partying, dining together, and paragraphs of glowing prose, extolling the virtues of a match made through the Sanford Dating Agency.

But Gemma had no eyes for the leaflet. Retracting the business card from the envelope slot into which it was placed, her heart began to pound.

"The boss wants to see you," Kibble told her. "Now."

"Yes," Gemma replied absently. "And I want to see him."

***

"Ever own one of those retractable dog leads, Murray?"

Joe remained cool in the light of Vickers' question. "Never owned a retractable dog."

Vickers felt his temper rising. "I'm warning you—"

"I run a café, Vickers. Food and dogs don't mix. Food and coppers trailing through the kitchen don't mix, either, as you'll find out when you finally drop this claptrap and I sue you."

"I'm investigating five murders—"

"No," Joe interrupted again. "You're trying to pin five murders on me and I don't have anything to do with them. But you're so pig-headed, so bloody determined that right now you're compromising my reputation and my business. You can't explain how my details got on the dating agency's database with the wrong picture, not because it's difficult to explain but because you won't accept that you're wrong. When I cracked that case in Wakefield I said you were an obstinate idiot, and I was right. Trouble is this time, Vickers, I'm not a dumb eighteen-year-old kid. I'm just as stubborn as you and you won't break me because I'm innocent."

Vickers half rose. A knock on the door prevented him losing his temper altogether. "In."

A police constable entered the interview room. While Vickers' partner muttered into the recorder, the constable said, "Sorry, sir, but Detective Sergeant Craddock is here."

Vickers nodded. "Interview terminated at..." he checked the time. "Thirteen-oh-five. Take Murray to the cells." He stormed from the room and confronted Gemma in the corridor. "You are in front of your station commander right now."

"Sir, I need to speak to you."

"I said now, Craddock." He marched along the corridor and Gemma hurried to keep up.

"Fine, whatever you want, sir, but I really need to speak to you first."

He stopped and rounded on her. "You have nothing to say that I want to hear. As far as I'm concerned, you've been meddling with this since the beginning in an effort to keep your uncle's name out of it. Going into the Sanford Dating Agency after you were suspended is the last straw. Now move it."

He marched off again and Gemma followed. "Your lookout."

"No, Craddock, it's yours."

***

Chief Superintendent Donald Oughton had been station commander for six years. Sanford born and raised, Gemma always felt he was a popular chief; one who let those below him get on with the job with the minimum of interference. But he was also a stickler for the rule book and while he listened to Vickers' tale, she could only sit, listen and fume at the injustice, while waiting for her say.

When the chief inspector had finished, Oughton turned concerned, blue-grey eyes on her. "I've know you a long time, Gemma. Ever since you were a probationer. You're a good copper; always have been. I've known Joe a great deal longer, and I find it hard to believe that he could commit these crimes, but I have to put personal considerations to one side. On the evidence, your uncle appears to be involved and when Chief Inspector Vickers removed you from the inquiry, you should have stayed away. You didn't, and he was right to suspend you. What's worse, you compounded that error by visiting the Sanford Dating Agency while suspended. Right now, you're facing a possible visit from Professional Standards, so you'd better come up with some pretty persuasive story to cover your actions."

Hand in her pocket, clinging tightly to the Sanford Dating Agency business card, Gemma drew in her breath. "My aim, sir, was to prevent a miscarriage of justice, and with all due respect, if Chief Inspector Vickers had listened to me in the corridor, we wouldn't be bringing this before you."

Vickers almost exploded. "How dare you—"

He was silenced by a raised finger from Oughton. "Let's hear Sergeant Craddock out, Chief Inspector."

"I admit, sir, I'm trying to clear my uncle's name but it's not because he's my uncle. It's because he's not guilty. I knew all along he wasn't guilty, and so did most of the town. Joe simply isn't like that. He was arrested this afternoon because his name appeared on the Sanford Dating Agency database. My inquiries, albeit carried out after I was suspended, have revealed that the Sanford Dating Agency is irrelevant."

Vickers fumed. "Each of those women had the Sanford Dating Agency business card in their possession."

"No, sir, they did not," Gemma snapped. "I saw only the card at Letty Hill's place. I haven't seen it from the other women, but the description fits all of them. A plain, white card with the initials SDA printed across the middle. That is not the Sanford Dating Agency card." She withdrew the business card from her pocket. "This is."

Vickers stared at the card, the background a pale lilac, its edges marked in an array of soft colours, the silhouette of a man and women printed inside a more familiar, rainbow arc. Across the middle was printed, *Sanford Dating Agency*, with two phone numbers beneath.

"I don't know what the other card is," Gemma admitted. "When we found it at Letty Hill's one of the officers told us it was the dating agency and we just accepted that. But it isn't."

Sweat broke on Vickers' brow. "It could be an old card—"

"No, sir," Gemma interrupted again. "I checked with Angela Foster. The basic design of her card has been the same for the last twenty years. There have been minor changes to it to accommodate more modern printing techniques, but it has never been a plain white card with just the initials on it."

A brief silence fell. Gemma and Oughton looked to Vickers. His eyes narrowed, brow creased and his lips moved soundlessly.

"Well, so it's not the dating agency, that doesn't mean Murray can't not have known them all."

"You're doing it again, sir," Gemma snapped. "You're determined to pin it on Joe. Forget him. He knew one of the victims; Letty Hill. There is nothing to suggest he knew any of the others. Nothing. There is nothing to suggest he was anywhere near Letty on the night she was murdered. You have no more right to throw this at him than you have any other man. Not without some supporting evidence, and right now you have nothing… Wrong. You do have something. A Joe Murray who'll be determined to crush you out of sight, and I know Joe. When he gets the bit between his teeth, he won't let go."

Another silence followed. This time Oughton broke it.

"I think Sergeant Craddock is right, Chief Inspector. I think you'd better release her uncle and make a statement to the press and TV to the effect that as of now, Joe Murray is no longer a suspect."

"This is not personal, sir," Gemma insisted. "I had no wish to embarrass Chief Inspector Vickers, and I did ask to speak to him before we came before you."

Thoroughly beaten, Vickers backed off. "You did, and, of course, you… you were right. I should have listened."

Silence fell. Vickers brow creased as if he were weighing his options. Gemma and Oughton waited for him to speak.

Eventually, he drew a deep and shuddery breath. "Chief Superintendent, in the light of this fresh evidence, I'm not sure that I'm the right man to take this investigation forward. I would suggest that you, first, reinstate Sergeant Craddock, and second, get onto the CC's office and ask for someone to replace me. Terry Cummins from York, or Ray Dockerty from Leeds, perhaps."

"I don't think that's necessary, Roy. This is just a hiccup and I'm sure Sergeant Craddock will not hold any of it against you." Oughton raised his eyebrow at Gemma and she concurred with a nod. "I think you've put so much into the investigation that you should see it through."

"It's not Gemma I'm concerned about, sir. It's her uncle. We all know Joe, and right now, he's mad as hell at me. He'll shove his nose in whether we like it or not, and it will be with the express intention of making me look a fool. That's not fair to the lads and lasses who've been working with me."

The superintendent smiled benignly. "Leave Joe Murray to me."

Chapter Eleven

"If you think Roy Vickers or the Sanford Police have heard the last of this, Don, you've another think coming. That bloody fool Vickers, dragged me out of my café not once but three times, and he did it in front of my staff and customers. What has that done to my reputation? How much business has it cost me? And that's not counting the cost of the damage he may have done walking in through the back door without wearing the proper gear."

In the face of Joe's anger, Oughton remained impassive, that faint, almost beatific smile playing at the corners of his mouth. When Joe fell silent, he leaned back in his executive chair, and glanced briefly through the window, out onto Gale Street.

Joe followed his gaze, out into the cold, February sunshine.

There were few people to be seen in this backwater. Gale Street was given over to police headquarters, magistrates' court, the offices of a few solicitors, accountants and other professionals, and some annexes of the Town Hall, but the rear entrance to The Gallery shopping centre, a reference to the town's mining past, could be seen from Oughton's office, and the few people who could be seen dodging the remaining patches of dirty snow, were hurrying towards the warmth of the mall. It was a part of the real world to which Joe fervently wanted to return.

"How long have we known each other, Joe?"

Oughton's question brought Joe back to reality of the superintendent's office. "What? Oh. I dunno. Fifty years?"

"Ever since primary school, eh?" Oughton laughed. "Nobody who went to that school ever forgot you and your gang. George Robson, Owen Frickley. You still hang out with 'em now, don't you?"

"They're members of the 3rd Age Club," Joe confirmed.

"Thieves, rogue and vagabonds." Oughton laughed again and as his laughter subsided, he became more wistful. "A lot of people in this town have cause to be grateful to you, Joe. As a private investigator, you have no equal. I don't know how much money you've saved local businesses solving their little problems without a fuss, and you've never take a penny from them."

"As long as they let me write them up," Joe concurred.

"By the same token, how much do you owe the Sanford police?"

Joe frowned. "As far as I know, nothing."

Oughton wagged a finger at him. "Ah, come on, Joe. That parking ticket Vinny Gillespie should have given you the other day is only the latest in blind eyes, and you know it. A bit of fly tipping here and there, getting rid of unwanted food where you shouldn't, MOT out of date on your car, a burglar alarm that kept crying wolf a few years back, dodgy tobacco bought from an even dodgier supplier, and I shudder to think how many times you've been nicked for an illegal lock-in with Mick Chadwick at the Miner's Arms. Not one, single prosecution. A ticking off at worst."

"Come off it, Don. I'm not the only one, and it's not like I ever dropped the police in it."

"Correct, and it's not like Roy Vickers has dropped you in it this time. He's on local TV as we speak, officially clearing you as a suspect. He'll also apologise personally."

"He already did." Joe leaned forward more aggressively. "But he was out to get me."

"I don't think so," Oughton disagreed. "Certainly, you're not his favourite person, but Roy is a professional police officer. He wouldn't let his antipathy towards you interfere with an investigation. He allowed himself to be misled by an error which was not his. The business card led us all to conclude that the Sanford Dating Agency was the key to this issue, and it's only thanks to your niece that we were shown the error of that approach. Roy has accepted he was wrong. He even offered to step down in favour of another chief inspector, but I refused to let him do it. What I'm saying to you, Joe, is that you should accept his apology in the spirit of sincerity with which it is offered and let's move on from there. And don't give me any flannel about cleaning your kitchen. If I sent Environmental Health round there, I'm willing to bet they'd find a lot more than policemen's muddy footprints."

"That's a bit below the belt, Don."

"No. It's an observation. I'll no more send Environmental Health than I'll pay you for your hurt feelings and extra floor mopping. You haven't lost any trade, either. In fact, if Gemma is to be believed, this business has boosted your custom. And Vickers got the *Sanford Gazette* to pull Rosemary Ecclesfield's piece on you before it ever went to press. Now come on, Joe. Let's call it a draw. In the spirit of friendship, I'm asking you to let it drop."

"Friendship? Me and Vickers?"

"No. You and me. You and the Sanford police."

Joe chewed spit. "You drive a hard bargain, Don."

The superintendent laughed. "Me and you both. We're Yorkshiremen, aren't we? Isn't it what we're best at; grinding the price down? Besides, I've no doubt you won't let the pursuit of the Sanford Valentine Strangler drop, and we may just need those eyes of yours." Oughton turned in his seat once more, and gazed through the window. "There's a killer somewhere out there, Joe. Four times he's struck, now. Five if you count Rosemary Ecclesfield. We need to get him and to do that, we need all the help we can get." He turned back and grinned. "Even if that help comes from a surly, miserable little toerag like you."

For the first time Joe, too, smiled. "If I want insults, all I have to do is stay at the Lazy Luncheonette." He got to his feet. "All right, Don. Fresh start. But, do me one favour. You're right; I'm not gonna let this case drop. I'll be pushing to find the Valentine Strangler. It's personal, remember. He murdered Letty Hill before I had the chance to get to know her better. I'll keep Vickers and his people posted on anything I turn up but, allow Gemma to keep me up to date with your end."

They shook hands.

"You have my word on it, Joe."

***

After picking up a photocopy of the SDA card common to the victims, Joe left the police station, made his way through The Gallery, out onto the market, crossed the square and entered the Sanford Dating Agency, where he found Angela Foster watching TV.

"Oh, Mr Murray. I've just been watching that Chief Inspector Vickers on TV. He says you were wrongly arrested and that you've now been officially cleared from the investigation."

"Correct," Joe replied, and picked up one of her leaflets. Waving it at her, he said, "And I have your business card to thank for it." He put the leaflet back into the display rack. "But you and I have a mutual problem, don't we?"

"Do we?"

"We do. How did my details, my photograph, get on your computer?"

She smiled. "The police say you put them on there."

Joe returned the smile but with more menace. "Then my guilt is not the only thing they've been wrong about, is it?"

The announcement, coupled to the gimlet gleam in Joe's eye, wiped the smile from her face. "I'm not, er, not sure what you mean."

"Let me put it in the simplest terms. I did not set up that account on your system. That means someone else did, and it would be helpful if we knew who."

Angela defended herself robustly. "Well, it wasn't me."

"I never said it was. But you need to get into your database, find out when it was set up, and that way we might just get a handle on it," Joe said. "And don't tell me it was done four years ago. It can't have been."

"In that case, you're out of luck, Mr Murray. I'm sure there must be ways of getting to the background source information, but I'm an administrator, not a computer geek, and I wouldn't have a clue where to begin."

Joe sighed. "All right. We'll leave it there for the time being. I may be back… or more likely, the police may be back. Now. What's the danger of my becoming a member of your dating site?"

Her face set prim, Angela replied, "I told you yesterday, I can't accept you."

"Yes, but my name's been cleared now."

"And I'm very happy for you. But it doesn't make you any better tempered than you were yesterday. The answer is no."

Feeling even more disgruntled in the light of her adamant refusal to accept him, Joe took a taxi from the market to the Lazy Luncheonette, where Sheila, Brenda and Cheryl were cleaning down after the day's trading.

They joined him for a cup of tea at table five, where he went through the day's events with them.

"At least you're in the clear, Joe," Sheila said.

Brenda gestured up at the large, wall-mounted TV opposite. "We saw Chief Inspector Vickers on telly. Humble pie? He looked like he needed new dentures to get through it."

"It still leaves us to find the Valentine Strangler," Joe pointed out.

"Yes, but aren't you better keeping out of it, Uncle Joe?"

Cheryl asked. "I mean, this bloke is dangerous."

Joe laughed harshly. "I'll give him dangerous if I get my hands on him."

"Hark at Arnold Swarthy Beggar," Brenda chuckled. "What you gonna do when you catch him, Joe? Throw a couple of steak and kidney pies at him?"

The doorbell rattled as Joe answered.

"I'll sick you onto him, Brenda." He looked up at the tall, grim-faced and bearded individual who had just walked in. "No food, pal. We're closing soon."

"No problem," the man replied. "I'm looking for Joe Murray."

Joe grinned. "If I owe you money I've never heard of him, if you owe me money, I'm your man."

To everyone's astonishment, the stranger grabbed Joe by the lapels and dragged him to his feet.

"Where are my mother's spoons?"

The three women leapt to intervene. Joe struggled to free himself of the man's grip. "Get your hands off me, you bloody idiot."

"Let him go!"

"Where are they, Murray?"

He shoved Joe back to the counter and pressed him back over it.

"Will someone get this moron off me?"

Brenda and Cheryl grabbed the stranger's arms in an effort to drag him off. He appeared not to notice.

"What have you done with them, Murray?"

Sheila hurried into the kitchen.

"I don't know what you're talking about," Joe gasped. "Now, for God's sake get off me."

"Leave him alone," Brenda screamed and dragged the stranger's arm again.

Sheila reappeared carrying a large knife. She held it in front of the man's eyes. "Take it," she insisted. "Take it and skewer him to the counter. Go on."

His eyes were fixed on the shining blade, hypnotised by it.

"While you're busy killing him, we'll call the police," Sheila went on. "So, go on. You're angry enough. Get rid of him for good if it'll make you feel any better."

He released Joe and stood back. Sheila returned the knife to the kitchen, and while Joe stood upright, shaking, his glare fastened on the newcomer, Sheila returned, and ordered, "Now, Mr Hill, why don't you sit down while we get you a cup of tea so we can talk calmly about your…what were they? Spoons?"

He backed further off and slumped into a seat. "How did you know my name?"

"An educated guess," Sheila replied. "I spent most of my life working as a school secretary, and I've seen many a child just as angry, as distressed as you. The only woman we know who was recently in Joe's life, was Letitia Hill, so it was obvious you were related to her. You're her son, aren't you?"

He nodded. "Tim Hill."

Aged about thirty, his beard neatly trimmed, he was smartly dressed in a dark overcoat and business suit beneath. His tie was tucked neatly under his chin, the pristine collar of a smart, white shirt, showing. Joe recognised Letty's eyes in him, but where hers had twinkled with laughter, his were empty.

"I got an early flight from Brussels this morning," he was saying, "and I've been at my mother's place all day." He appeared completely deflated, on the verge of tears. "Someone stole her Regency spoons."

"Well, it wasn't me," Joe snapped. He rounded on Sheila. "And what the hell were you doing offering him a knife to kill me with?"

"I told you, I know distressed children, and it doesn't matter how old they are, they're still mothers' sons. I knew it would snap him out of it." Sheila sat with Tim. "Get him a cup of tea, Brenda." She took his hand. "Tim, we're all very sorry about Letitia, but Joe had nothing to do with her death. Did you not see the police broadcast earlier?"

"Yes. Yes I did." He took a cup of tea from Brenda, and loosened his topcoat. "Someone took her spoons. I want them back. I guessed it was him because he was the last one to see her alive."

"If anyone took Letty's spoons, it was the cops," Joe argued. "They were still there on Friday when they found your mother."

Accepting a beaker of sweet tea from Brenda, Tim shook his head. "That particular set of spoons is still there, Murray. But they're not the originals. They're cheap copies. Worth nothing at all."

"So you're an expert on Regency cutlery are you?" Joe snapped.

He shook his head again. "No. But I grew up with those spoons. They were a family heirloom passed on from generation to generation. I was taking them back to Brussels, but the moment I looked at them, I knew they weren't the real ones." He stared at Joe. His eyes had lost most of their anger, and were now filled only with sadness. "When I spoke to Mother on the phone on Thursday, she said she'd met you, and she'd been telling you all about her and Dad. I just assumed… I'm sorry. I'm not normally so quick-tempered."

"Bloody spoons," Joe grumbled. "What do I know about spoons? I wouldn't know the difference between Regency silver and Korean plate."

"I said I'm sorry," Tim responded. "The police insist that the killer hadn't taken or disturbed anything, so I thought the switch had been made before her death, and since you were the last man to see her, I naturally…" He broke down and began to weep. "I'm sorry."

Brenda moved to the table and helped Sheila to comfort the distraught man. Joe sat across the aisle feeling guilty, then reproved himself. He had nothing to feel guilty about.

Cheryl tapped Joe's arm. "Uncle Joe, I have to go. Mum will be expecting me to pick up Danny."

He gave a grouchy smile. "You get going, Cheryl. We'll see you tomorrow, chicken." As she left, he concentrated on Tim. "How can you be so certain these spoons have been switched?"

Tim drew a breath to control his emotions, then took another swallow of tea. "The case. I spotted it right away. It's covered in blue velvet, and you couldn't tell from the colour, but the corners are wrong. They're square. Right angled. On mother's, they were rounded. Then I checked the spoons. Huh." He sneered. "EPNS. Made in Sheffield. I can buy them on eBay for less than twenty pounds."

The gears in Joe's brains began to mesh. "Have you told the police any of this?"

"No." He sighed. "I should have done. I should have gone to them before I came here. How many times do I have to say I'm sorry?"

"No, no. It's no problem. There's no real harm done."

Sheila and Brenda exchanged a furtive glance. Brenda concentrated on Joe. "I've seen that look on your face before, Joe Murray. What's going through that devious mind of yours?"

"Means, motive and opportunity," Joe replied. He took out his tobacco and began to roll a cigarette. "Gemma told me that a neighbour heard a car pull up outside Letty's place on the night she died. It was there for about an hour. They assume that this was when your mother was murdered... Tim, I'm sorry if this is distressing."

Tim shook his head once more and, in a flat tone of resigned acceptance, said, "Please go on. If it gets the police any closer to my mother's killer, I'll listen."

"Right," Joe agreed. "In all four killings the police have assumed the motive was sex. They get that from the way the victims were left, laid on the bed and... well, you know what I mean. The odd thing is, none of the victims had been sexually assaulted." He noticed Tim shudder and apologised again. "I'm sorry to put you through this, lad. Suppose the police have it wrong?" He grunted. "It wouldn't be the first time in this case, would it? Suppose the victims were left like that to lead the police on; make them *think* it was a sex killing. Suppose the motive was something else. Something entirely different."

Brenda's eyes lit up. "Like substituting genuine antiques with fake ones?"

"Correct."

Silence fell. Joe knew they were turning the idea over in their minds, just the way he was, looking for the flaws.

"No, no, it can't be," Sheila said. "The families would notice, wouldn't they? Just as Tim has."

"Would they?" Joe faced the distraught man. "Tim, was it the case that drew your attention to the spoons?"

Tim nodded. "I told you; I noticed it right away."

"So if they had been in the original case, say, or one similar, how long would it have taken you to spot the switch?"

Tim shrugged. "I don't know. Months. Years. Maybe never. I wasn't going to sell them. I was just going to take them back to Brussels. They're a family heirloom."

"My point precisely," Joe declared. "Sheila, you have some clown statuette, don't you? Worth a mint."

"*Pagliaccio*," Sheila concurred. "It's worth a couple of thousand pounds. Maybe more."

"Right, now bear with me," Joe insisted. "If, God forbid, something happened to you, and someone switched your china figure for a fake, would Aaron or Peter Junior notice?"

She was hesitant. "I don't know. In my case, probably, because they would be entitled to split the value, so they would more than likely sell it. But I take your point. If it's a family heirloom handed down from generation to generation, like Letty's spoons, and the object had no, er, case, like Tim's the family may not spot the switch."

"But," Brenda objected, "did the other victims have such heirlooms?"

"They were all middle class women, for want of a better description," Joe pointed out, "so the odds are high."

"Even if you're right, Murray," Tim pointed out, "it still doesn't tell you who the police are looking for."

Joe reached into his pocket and took out the photocopy he had been given at the police station. "No, but this might help narrow it down."

They all craned to look at the copy. Sheila's colour drained.

"Oh, no."

All eyes turned on her.

"What?" Joe demanded. "What is it?"

Her hand shaking, she dug into her purse and came out with a matching card. Laying it on the table, alongside the photocopy, she said, "SDA. Stewart Dalmer Antiques."

Chapter Twelve

"You were right, Murray," Vickers said. "I don't know how you got there, but you called it spot on."

It was eleven o'clock the following morning. Joe had phoned Gemma the moment Sheila confirmed Stewart Dalmer was the owner of the mysterious business card, and after overnight activity from the police, Vickers had phoned Joe half an hour previously, inviting him to Gale Street, where, with Gemma joining them, the chief inspector delivered the news.

Reading from a printout, Vickers said, "Fiona temple owned a Victorian tea caddy finished in faux tortoiseshell. It was worth about four hundred pounds. Her daughter has it now. Bridget Ackroyd owned a matching silver, cream jug and sugar bowl, worth about eight hundred pounds. That's with her eldest son. The biggest score was Thelma Warburton. She owned a pair of Japanese Satsuma plates, dated from about 1800. They were worth three thousand pounds. After she was killed, her son and daughter put them up for sale, so they could split the difference, only to learn that they were cheap copies, worth maybe fifty pounds."

"And they didn't complain?" Joe asked.

The chief inspector shook his head. "They just assumed that their mother had been telling them tall tales about the value of the plates. We've taken the other two items, the tea caddy and Victorian silverware to a specialist in Leeds and we're waiting for his verdict, but when two out of the four have been switched, it's odds on those will be fakes, too."

"And what about Dalmer?" Joe asked.

"We're treading lightly," Gemma said. "The card strengthens our suspicions, obviously. We've tried the number and only got voicemail."

"Sheila told me he never answers the phone," Joe reported. "He told her it was to avoid the conmen in the antiques game, but that's just an excuse."

"It sounds reasonable on the face of it," Vickers ventured.

Joe grunted. "To someone who's never been in business, it would, but when Sheila told me, I knew straight away what his game was."

"You can't just come right out and accuse people of murder, Uncle Joe," Gemma tutted.

"At the risk of starting another argument, you didn't hesitate with me." Joe pressed on before Vickers could pick him up. "Besides, I'm not accusing Dalmer of murder. I'm accusing him of dodging the tax man."

Both officers stared.

"I sell meals, right? The food has to be top notch or I don't want to know, so I don't buy off the back of a lorry. I've read of restaurants buying unlabelled cans only to learn that they contain Pedigree Chum. So I don't do it. But take Dennis who runs the DIY shop next door to me. When some guy turns up and asks if he wants a load of timber left over from a job, the only question Dennis asks is, 'how much'. Dalmer can't do that. He buys from householders, and very often, they won't make a decision there and then. So he needs to give them some means of contacting him, but he doesn't want word to spread too far that he's in the game, and by too far, I mean the tax and VAT offices. So he produces a plain business card bearing only the initials and a mobile phone number. Five'll get you ten, if you trace the number, it'll be registered in a false name—"

"It is," Vickers interrupted. "Albert Rawmarsh."

Joe chuckled. "I thought Rawmarsh was near Rotherham.

Right, so he has this card and phone number that can't easily be tracked to him. If HMRC get onto him, he can deny everything. It's up to the tax man then to prove he's making money and owes them. You see?"

"Complicated," Gemma said.

"Worth it," Joe argued. "Between the tax and the bloody VAT I'm surprised I stay in business."

"Forget tax and VAT and tell us about Dalmer," Vickers invited.

"What's to tell?" Joe took out his tobacco tin and began to roll a cigarette while he formulated his thoughts. "I don't know the man that well. He used to be a teacher at Sanford Tech, and I know he's into antiques. Snooty, you know. Drinks in some arty-farty pub in Wakefield. The Artesian Well. All they talk about is Dostoevsky, Rimski-Korsakov and post-impressionism. He's stood against me for the Chair of the 3rd Age Club a couple of times, but the members don't want him. His idea of an outing is a visit to the Ashmolean or the British Library." Joe frowned and tucked the completed cigarette in his shirt. "I wouldn't have said he was a serial killer but hell, what do I know? I will tell you this, though; there's something that doesn't quite add up here."

"What's that?" Gemma asked.

"I dunno," Joe admitted, "but it'll come to me eventually. When it does, I'll bell you." He fished into his gilet, seeking his Zippo lighter. "You'll be bringing him in?"

"Definitely," Vickers agreed. "He's the only connection we have between the four women."

"Tread carefully," Joe advised. "Don Oughton might have been able to talk me out of suing you, but I wouldn't bet he can do the same with Stewart Dalmer." He stood up. "Right, if there's nothing else, I've a business to run. If I think of anything, I'll let you know."

From the police station, throughout the drive along icy roads, something nagged at Joe. It was always the way.

Somewhere in the flurry of information over the last few days, something tiny, something apparently insignificant had been lodged in his head and now that he wanted it, he could not retrieve it.

The key, he knew, was to engage his mind elsewhere. As a consequence, when he stepped through the back door into the Lazy Luncheonette's kitchen, and found Sheila absent, he put on his whites, and walked into the café, just as the lunchtime trade was picking up.

"Where's Sheila?" he asked.

"The police rang. Her alarm is going off and they found the door open," Brenda replied. "I told her to get on home and sort it. Cheryl and I can cope."

Joe stationed himself behind the counter. "You don't need to now, do you? The boss is back."

Brenda looked around, and then grinned. "Boss? Where?"

***

Sheila braked sharply outside her house, and yanked the handbrake on.

After a call from the police and an anxious journey from the Lazy Luncheonette, there was no sign of a patrol car. "Typical," she muttered.

Her irritation rising, she stared along the path at the side of her bungalow, where she could see the door open. Above the front windows, the blue light of the alarm flashed, its screamer now silenced.

"You'd think they would have had the decency to wait," she growled at her car.

Frowning irritably she climbed out and hurried along the path and into the hall. "Hello," she called out.

Behind her, the door slammed shut. She whirled around and found herself staring down the barrel of a pump action shotgun.

"Good afternoon, Mrs Riley. Let's go into the living room, shall we? We may have a while to wait."

***

The time was coming up to two, and with the afternoon lull setting in, Joe sat at table five, leaving the few customers to Brenda and Cheryl, while he ran over and over the events of the day.

"Trouble at t' mill?" Brenda asked, joining him.

"What? Oh. Hmm, yeah. There's something not right about all this, Brenda."

"Stewart, you mean? Well, Joe, there's no accounting for folk, is there? We only see what's on the outside. We can never know what's going on behind the façade." She yawned. "It's like looking at a photograph. We see what the camera sees, but we don't know what's going on inside, do we?"

The light bulb lit in Joe's head. "As usual, you've done it, Brenda. Hit the nail on the head." He snatched up his mobile and dialled.

"What nail?" Brenda asked.

He shushed her and called up the photographs on his phone. Highlighting the one used on Angela Foster's database, he brought it to the screen and angled the phone so both he and Brenda could see.

His face filled most of the image, his eyes shaded by the peak of his flat cap. Above his head was a dark triangle filling the top left corner. Joe pointed to it.

"What does that look like?"

Brenda shrugged. "I dunno. A building of some sort?"

"Or maybe the top corner of a market stall? You know. Where the roof comes over," Joe suggested.

"Hmm. Could be."

"No could be about it." He cleared the screen, called up the directory, selected Gemma's number, and hit the connect button. A moment later he was through. "Gemma? It's Joe. Did you bring Stewart Dalmer in?"

"The boss is grilling him now," Gemma reported.

"Progress?"

"Tough, Uncle Joe," she replied. "He's admitted everything but the murders. Says he's innocent."

"And he is," Joe insisted. "Ask yourself about the photograph of me on the Sanford Dating Agency database. How could Dalmer get hold of it?"

"Well, I suppose… well, I don't know, do I? Has he had access to the 3rd Age Club database?"

"No, and even if he had, it wouldn't do him any good. That's not my 3rd Age Club ID picture. I think the photograph was taken on Sanford Market on Monday and it's one of Rosemary Ecclesfield's. Do you have the downloads from her camera?"

There was a pause. "Yes. I'm sure we do."

"Dig 'em out," Joe insisted. "I'm on my way now." He cut the connection, and moved to the kitchen to collect his coat. "Cash up will you, please, Brenda. I'll bell you later."

For the second time in the space of a few hours, Joe drove into Sanford, but more hurriedly this time, irritably cursing every crawling driver on the road. He rushed into Gemma's department just after two fifteen, and she had all the photographs displayed as thumbnails on her computer screen.

"What's all this about, Joe?" she demanded.

Joe sat alongside her and scanned the images. There were about two hundred; mostly of him, his car, or the Lazy Luncheonette, but eventually he found the image he had been seeking; a fuller replica of the one on the Sanford Dating Agency database.

"That is what it's all about," he declared. "Rosemary Ecclesfield took that photograph on Monday morning while I was waiting for the Sanford Dating Agency doors to open. She obviously never downloaded it from the camera, so how the hell did it get onto Angela Foster's system?"

Gemma thought about it. "We know Rosemary cooked up a story about you and she was missing from about three o'clock that afternoon. Perhaps Angela was in on it."

"Then you'd better tackle her," Joe said. "Gemma, don't take this the wrong way, but there is another possibility."

She raised her eyebrows. "What?"

"Who unloaded the camera onto your database?"

"Well, I think… probably Des Kibble, or maybe Paul Ingleton. I don't know, but it won't take long to find out."

Joe's mobile chirped for attention. "You see what I'm driving at?" he asked Gemma. "Anyone in this station could have had access to it."

"Come off it, Uncle Joe. I know Roy Vickers doesn't like you, but he wouldn't—"

"I'm not talking about Vickers, but anyone. Anyone who might want to cover up his activities by blaming me. And think about it, Gemma. You said the Valentine Strangler never leaves a trace in the victims' houses. Who would be the best at covering his tracks? A police officer in a forensic jump suit, that's who."

His phone continued to ring. Reading *Brenda* in the menu, he made the connection.

"Yeah, Brenda. What's up, sugar?"

She sounded worried. "It's Sheila. I tried ringing her and I can't get an answer."

"Well, maybe she's busy with the police."

"That wouldn't stop her answering the phone. What if something's happened to her, Joe?"

Joe sighed. "All right. I'll go there next. Stop worrying, Brenda. I'll bell you from Sheila's. She'll be all right. You'll see." He cut the connection and concentrated on Gemma. "Sorry, kid, but staff welfare calls."

"What's the problem?" Gemma asked.

"One of your people rang Sheila earlier and told her she'd

had a break in."

"Hmm. First I've heard of it."

Joe laughed and gestured at the photographs. "You have more on your plate. I'll get going. Let me know if you come up with anything."

***

With Joe gone, Gemma began to work on the photographs. Within minutes, her intense concentration had turned to a frown of worry.

She called up other files, and found she was denied access to them. She cut along to reception. "Where's Des Kibble?"

"Out," the constable on duty reported. "Burglary or something."

"Where?"

The youngster shrugged. "Sorry, Sarge, I dunno."

Gemma speared him with a glare. "Then find out, idiot."

Face glowing red, the young constable turned from the counter and consulted the CID signing book.

"Sixteen Larch Avenue," he reported. "Name of Riley."

Gemma frowned. "Who reported it?"

He checked the records again. "Doesn't seem to have come through here, Sarge. Someone must have called him direct."

Gemma's blood ran cold. "Oh my God, no." Gazing frantically around, seeing Vinny Gillespie heading for the exit, she barked at the reception constable, "Sign me out to the same address. Vinny. Come on."

Gillespie looked surprised. "Me? I was just on me way home, Sarge."

"You're on overtime. Come on. It's an emergency."

Spurred by her orders, Gillespie followed her out to the rear car park where they climbed into his patrol car.

"Blue lights, siren, the works," Gemma ordered.

"Where to?"

"Sixteen Larch Avenue. Sheila Riley's place. Move it, Vinny."

As the car tore out into the streets, Gemma rang Joe and got no answer. She tried again, and then a third time.

"No answer. Typical Joe. Won't answer the bloody phone when he's driving. Vinny. Step on it."

While the car lurched, swayed and sped along the busy streets, Gemma dialled the station and after a brief argument with the desk, finally got through to Vickers.

"What the hell is it, Craddock?" the chief inspector demanded. "I'm in the middle of questioning Dalmer."

"It's not him, sir. It's Des Kibble."

The announcement was greeted with a brief silence, followed by an explosive, incredulous, "What?"

"He collects antiques, sir, and the woman he was involved with in Bradford? She disappeared just after Valentine's Night. Maybe there was some truth in the rumours." Frantically she garbled on, leaving Vickers no choice but to listen. "Think about it, sir. He can move around without leaving any trace of himself, and now he's called Sheila Riley out to a burglary that no one but him seems to know about. I'm on my way there now with Constable Gillespie."

"I'll release Dalmer on bail. Keep me informed."

***

Much the same thoughts occupied Joe's mind as he weaved his way through the outer suburban streets of Sanford, but he was less centred on Kibble, thinking more of the police in general.

With hindsight, everything pointed to a forensic officer, one sufficiently skilled and in possession of the necessary equipment to let him hide all traces of himself. Antiques pointed at Kibble, but less than twenty-four hours earlier, they had pointed at Stewart Dalmer, and before that, other factors had been aimed at him.

It could, he admitted to himself, be any one of twenty or thirty officers.

Turning into Larch Avenue, seeing the dark Ford parked outside number twelve, he changed his mind. It was Kibble.

Pulling further down, parking ahead of Sheila's compact Fiat, he sat behind the wheel for a moment, debating with himself how best to approach the problem.

Sheila's silence was explained. Kibble had lured her here and, for all Joe knew, she could already be dead, strangled like the others.

He was surprised by the pain and anger that thought sent through him. He, Sheila, Brenda and the likes of George Robson and Owen Frickley had been the best of friends since the schoolyard, but he had never felt any particular attachment to any of them. He'd dated Brenda for a while as a teenager, and he would defend the two women to the last if he had to, but beyond that, there had never been any emotional ties to either of them. And yet, the thought of her dead, or worse, *murdered*, hurt.

It also annoyed him. Kibble, he knew, was still in the house. Should he charge in there, hold him, make a citizen's arrest until the police arrived?

Joe, even as a kid you couldn't punch your way out of a paper bag.

Brenda's words came back to haunt him. It was the truth. He had never been a scrapper, and Kibble was at least twenty years younger than him.

Even so, he could not let the man simply walk away after another murder.

He made up his mind, climbed out of the car, opened the boot and took out his wheel brace. A chrome-plated, telescopic handle, about eighteen inches long, it was made of mild steel, and it would be more than adequate to deal with Des Kibble.

Filled with fresh determination and anger, he marched up the garden path and rapped on the door.

"Come on out, Kibble. I know you're in there."

Nothing happened. Joe tried the door and to his surprise found it unlocked. He pushed it open and walked cautiously in, his wheel brace at the ready.

He crept along the hall to the open living room door. "I'm warning you, Kibble, I'm armed."

He turned into the room and stopped dead, staring at a shotgun aimed at his chest.

A broad grin backed up the gun. "Armed, are you? Well so am I."

***

Siren still blaring, Gillespie's car screamed into Larch Avenue and came to a screeching halt behind Kibble's vehicle. Almost as it stopped, Gemma leapt out, one eye on the ageing estate car a few spaces ahead.

"Joe's here already," she said, hurrying along the pavement and turning into Sheila's gate.

She stopped dead as one of the front windows opened and Joe, looking terrified, leaned out.

"Get lost, Gemma. Just go away. This guy means business."

As if to reinforce the message, the barrel of a shotgun appeared alongside him.

"Go," Joe urged his niece. "Get out of here, girl. Now."

***

It took less than half an hour to get Vickers, Oughton and an armed response unit to the street.

Gemma and Gillespie had backed off, away from the house, and while waiting for reinforcements, they had manned each end of the street, preventing other vehicles from entering.

When the team arrived, she crouched with Vickers and Oughton in the shelter of a patrol car, and briefed them.

"I don't know for certain who's in there, sir, other than Uncle Joe and one man armed with what looked like a pump action shotgun. Mrs Riley's car is there, so, too, is Kibble's. I don't know if Mrs Riley is still alive, but I'm betting it's Kibble behind the shotgun."

"Guess again, Sergeant," Vickers suggested, and handed a couple of sheets of computer printouts to her.

Gemma read them with amazement. "I don't believe it."

Vickers shrugged. "What's not to believe? Came home on Valentine's Night ten years ago, found his wife with another man. Des Kibble. Three days later, his wife walked out on him. Never been seen since. Remember what I told you about tongues wagging behind Des's back?"

"They should have been wagging behind *his* back," Gemma grumbled.

"True," Vickers agreed, "but he wasn't a cop then. He didn't join the service until two years after that."

The sergeant in charge of the ARU scurried to join them. "All exits covered, sir. He won't get out."

"Can you get at him through the windows?" Oughton demanded.

The sergeant shook his head. "First off, sir, they're sealed units, double glazed. As if that's not bad enough, the outer panes are leaded. If we hit the lead anywhere on the pattern, it may deflect the bullet, and there's no telling where it might end up. Finally, he has Joe Murray stood with his back to the window. We couldn't guarantee not hitting Joe." Grim-faced, the sergeant went on, "We could try taking out the doors, but he'd have enough time to kill one or all his hostages, depending on how many he has, or alternatively, he could be waiting for our boys to walk in and open up on them."

"If that's a legal pump action, it can only hold three cartridges," Oughton pointed out.

"We have no way of knowing whether it's legal, Don," Vickers pointed out. "Our only hope is to negotiate with him."

Still reading the reports, Gemma tapped Vickers on the shoulder. "Sir, how come Kibble never made the connection between his girlfriend and our man? I mean if they were married—"

"I checked when you rang me," Vickers interrupted. "Des was questioned when the woman disappeared. He knew her by her maiden name. Ainsworth. Not Ingleton."

Chapter Thirteen

Joe's shock at facing the shotgun soon settled to surprise when he saw the face behind it. Dressed, as Joe had anticipated, in forensic overalls, it was not Des Kibble but Paul Ingleton.

Herded into the living room, he found Kibble backed against the rear wall, near to Sheila's display cabinet of fine china, while Sheila herself, was tied to a dining room chair, her skirt pushed up, underwear on show. Both the fingerprint man and Sheila appeared terrified.

The display cabinet was open, and on the highly polished dining table stood the Meissen figurine of *Pagliaccio*. Joe had no doubt that Ingleton would have a copy of it somewhere.

Joe had never been so frightened. His mind, normally so agile, so quick to respond to any situation, froze and all he could think of was death.

Standing in the centre of the room, next to Sheila, his hands raised, he tried to speak, but no sound would come. Swallowing hard, he cleared his throat and opened his mouth.

At that moment, Vinny Gillespie's car screamed to a halt outside. Ingleton checked, saw Gemma hurrying towards the house, and motioned Joe to the window.

"Tell them to get away," he ordered. The shotgun swung erratically on Sheila and Kibble. "Move and I'll blow you away: both of you."

Joe did as he was told. He was too scared to do anything but. When Gemma and Gillespie ran, Ingleton ordered Joe to stand with his back to the window.

"You've screwed everything up, Murray," he complained.

"Now I have to think how to handle this." He glared at Kibble. "I think you're gonna have to shoot him. Before you shoot yourself."

The fingerprint man shook his head. "I'm shooting no one."

With a smug, superior smile, Ingleton tutted. "You forget, Des, I work in forensics, too. Do you think I can't strangle her, shoot him, then you, and not have the ability to make it look like you did it?"

Joe cleared his throat again. "That's, er, that's what you've been doing all along, isn't it?" he jerked a thumb at Kibble. "Trying to make it look like he did it."

"Four women," Ingleton hissed. "Five if you count the reporter. And all because he couldn't keep his hands off my wife."

"I didn't know she was your wife," Kibble pleaded. "She told me she was single."

"Liar!" Ingleton snapped. "You think I'd believe that? You saw all the photographs of me in the house. You must have done. You knew she was married."

"There were no photographs and she told me her name was Ainsworth."

"You're a liar, Kibble."

Still frightened, Joe lowered his hands and shook his head. "No. He's telling it like it is, and you know it, Ingleton. And I'll bet Kibble wasn't the first or the only one."

The shotgun whirled on Joe. "Don't you talk about her like that. You didn't know her."

Trembling, terrified that his next words might be his last, Joe decided he had nothing to lose by doing what he had done all his life: tell it like it was.

"Let's be honest about this. Including Letty Hill, you've murdered four women, always on or around Valentine's Night. If you'd wanted to pin it on Kibble, you'd have done it before now. I think you substituted the antiques to make it look as if it was Kibble or even Stewart Dalmer, but you murdered those women for your own purposes. Getting off?" Joe raised his eyebrows. "Or getting even?"

The usual, easygoing smile of the police photographer was gone, and in its place was a mask of bubbling anger. The façade of the injured, grieving husband began to crumble and when he spoke it was in tones of pure acid.

"Bitches! All of them. Bitches on heat." He bit the words off. With the shotgun wavering between his three hostages, he pressed on in a hiss filled with bile. "I was in Iraq and Afghanistan. I saw some of my mates shot up so badly, their bodies were unrecognisable. I helped pick up the pieces of buddies who had been blown to hell by roadside booby traps. And what was she doing while I was over there, fighting for my country? Fooling around with lowlife like him."

"I'm sorry about that," Joe said. "It must have hurt. But did that give you the right to take it out on these other women?"

"They're all the same," Ingleton shouted. "Give 'em an inch, they'll take a mile. Even miss purity here." He waved the shotgun at Sheila and she cringed. "Oh I don't bother with men. I'm preserving the memory of my dearly departed husband. Who put him in his grave, eh? Her." Now he gestured manically at the room. "Keeping up with the Joneses. Sending him out to work so she could keep the House Beautiful, until he worked himself into an early grave. Women. They're all alike. They don't deserve to live."

"I, er…" Joe's mind worked frantically. He could see that Ingleton was close to breaking point, and needed something to bring him back. "What is this Valentine thing with you? Pushing their skirts up like that? You just like looking at knickers, do you? Hang around in the underwear department in big shops, maybe?"

The gun waved his way again. "Careful, Murray." Ingleton seemed to relax a little. "When do you think I found the bitch?"

For a moment, Joe had to wonder which bitch, but he soon put it together. "Oh. Your wife. Valentine's Night and she was laid on the bed with her skirt up showing her clouts?"

"The only difference was she had no clouts on. She'd just been with him."

Joe tried to be nonchalant. He had seen many a movie hero so relaxed in this kind of situation and he wondered why he couldn't be the same.

"Ah. I think I get it, now. You could never touch her again, could you? Or any other woman, come to that. So when you strangled the other women, it was always on Valentine's Night, or as close as you could get, and you left their knickers on to cover up what you could never go near again." He scowled. "You're sick."

"Better sick than dead."

More afraid than ever, all Joe could do was keep him talking. "And the card and paper flower?" Joe realised at once the answer to his question. "Of course. You had a card and paper flower for your missus that night, didn't you? So how did you know about Sheila's *Pagliaccio* statuette and all the other antiques?"

"Your pal, Dalmer. He has a big mouth. We drink in the same pub in Wakefield. The Artesian Well."

"Arty-farty," Joe muttered.

"You would think that," Ingleton snapped. "You wouldn't know the difference between Crown Derby and the Crown and Anchor. Course, Dalmer doesn't know me. Not by name, anyway. To him, I'm just Paul. A regular guy, just like him, interested in antiques."

"And that's how you found out about them all?" Joe shook his head. "I don't believe you. No way would he give you their addresses. He'd see you as a competitor."

"He didn't have to, you idiot. I'm a cop. You think I can't track people? All I needed was a name and I could find them." Kibble snapped his fingers. "That easy."

"Really? You got my address wrong."

The policeman sneered. "I was in a hurry. And I am now. I can't stand around here chatting all day, Murray. Things to do, people to see, *Pagliaccio* figurines to exchange, you three to shine on. See you in heaven… or hell."

He squeezed the trigger and Joe closed his eyes expecting nothing but death.

A loud, electronically amplified voice boomed through the silence. "Ingleton. This is Chief Superintendent Oughton. We have the place surrounded, and we have armed officers with their sights trained on all exits. Remove the shells from your shotgun, put it down outside where we can see it, and come out with your hands raised."

***

Having heard nothing from Sheila or Joe, Brenda left Cheryl with the keys to the Lazy Luncheonette, and drove out to Sheila's. They had been friends since school, and if Sheila was in trouble, it was her duty to help.

It was a complete shock when she ran into a road block at the corner of Sheila's quiet street, and found the area swarming with armed police.

"But I'm Mrs Riley's best friend," she told Gillespie on the barricade.

"I'm sorry, luv," said Gillespie, "but I can't let you past."

"Is Gemma here? Gemma Craddock?"

"Natch."

"Get her here, Vinny," Brenda ordered.

Gillespie spoke into his radio, and a few moments later, Gemma, wearing a flak jacket and crouching low, came to the barricade.

"Our spotters are concentrated on the house and we have the place surrounded, Mrs Jump," Gemma explained. "Someone has them at gunpoint in the living room."

Brenda's features paled in the waning sunlight. "Oh, my God, no. But... but... is there anything I can do, Gemma?"

"Yes, there is. Keep out of the way. We're talking to neighbours trying to get an idea of the layout inside Mrs Riley's house."

Brenda beamed. "Forget the neighbours. Get me a bulletproof vest like yours and I'll draw you a plan."

Gemma was surprised. "You know it well?"

"I was maid of honour at Sheila's wedding."

Gemma removed her body armour and handed it over. "Keep your head down as we move along the street," she ordered. "I dunno. Between you and Uncle Joe and Mrs Riley, you'll get me fired."

***

Joe risked a glance through the window where several police cars crowded the narrow street. A look of panic spread across Ingleton's face.

Joe tried to smile. "Looks like your disappearing act is cancelled, Ingleton."

"Shut up!" sweat broke on Ingleton's forehead. He backed off towards the rear wall, where it would be more difficult for the police outside to see him. "Right now, Murray, I still have the upper hand. I have you three and they won't risk your lives."

The loudhailer boomed again.

"Paul, this is Roy Vickers. We know everything, buddy. We know you're holding Des Kibble, Mrs Riley and Murray at gunpoint, and you should realise we're not going away. You can't escape, lad. Put the gun down and come out. No one's going to hurt you if you do as you're told."

"He's right, and you know it," Kibble muttered, and cowered as Ingleton waved the shotgun again.

"If you don't go out," Joe said, "they'll come in."

"It'll be bad news for you three if they do."

***

Out in the street, crouched in the shelter of a police car, Vickers and Oughton were in urgent conference with the sergeant in charge of the armed unit who studied Brenda's rough drawing of the interior. Close by, Gemma and Brenda listened.

"Right now, sir, Ingleton is stood well back," the sergeant reported, "and no one has a clear shot at him. If this lady's drawing is correct, we could go in through the back door and have him pinned in seconds, but as I said earlier, we'll have trouble getting through the door without alarming him."

"What about storming the place, both doors at the same time?" Oughton asked.

The sergeant grimaced. "Same problem, sir. By the time we smash the door down, Ingleton could shoot the hostages, or he could easily get himself into a position where he would take out our people as they go in."

"Suppose you had a key and you could sneak in?" Brenda asked.

The police scowled at her.

"You've done well, luv, giving us this map, but don't tell me you also know the locksmith who set the doors up?" the sergeant demanded.

"No," said Brenda, dipping into her purse. "But Sheila and I have been best friends since before you were born." She dangled a key before them. "This fits her back door." She smiled. "Sheila has the key to my place, too. It's for when one of us is ever unwell."

"You're sure you can get to him from the rear?" the chief inspector asked.

"As long as we can get in quietly, yes, sir," The sergeant confirmed. "I have people round there already, sir, and

Ingleton can't see them from the living room." He took the key from Brenda.

"No shooting unless it's absolutely necessary," Oughton insisted. "Remember, there are three innocent people in there."

***

Back in the house, Joe felt sufficiently emboldened to begin untying Sheila.

Ingleton swung the shotgun back on him. "What the hell do you think you're doing?"

"You just said that if they decide to storm the place, you're going to kill all of us before they kill you," Joe grumbled. "If Sheila has to die, she'll die with dignity, not showing next week's washing like you left those other women."

"Thank you, Joe," Sheila said as he removed her gag. "I'm sorry to have dragged you into this, but he threatened to shoot me, the coward."

"No problem, Sheila," Joe assured her as he released her bonds. "Besides, it was Brenda who dragged me into it, and what am I here for if not to intervene in life or death situations?"

She stood up, smoothed her skirt down, and turned virulent eyes on Ingleton. "You're a disgrace to the uniform."

"I'm not uniformed," Ingleton sneered gruffly.

"Don't split hairs," Sheila snapped. "You are a disgrace to the police service. My husband served this community all his life and never once did he—"

The erratic detective swung angrily on her, the shotgun coming round. Joe grabbed her by the arm, yanked her to floor, and followed her down, laying himself half over her. By the rear wall, Kibble, too, hit the deck.

At the same time there came a cry from the kitchen as armed officers came in through the back door. Ingleton turned to face the door, waiting for them to rush in. With the photographer's back turned, Joe spotted the opportunity, leapt to his feet and grabbed the first thing he could lay hands on. Sensing the movement, Ingleton was turning Joe's way again, when Joe brought the Meissen *Pagliaccio* down on his head. The porcelain figure broke, Ingleton crumpled to the carpet, the shotgun discharged a single cartridge into the wall, and three armed officers appeared, in the room, their guns aimed at Joe.

He let the remains of *Pagliaccio* drop and raised his hands. "I'm one of the good guys."

From the floor, Sheila screamed in horror. "Joe Murray, that was genuine Meissen, worth over two thousand pounds."

Joe winced and smiled obsequiously. "Meissen? You're sure it wasn't Mason?

Chapter Fourteen

Joe awoke in the dim light of morning straining through dark, blood-red curtains. His head pounded, his tongue was furred up, and he didn't have a clue where he was but it was not his flat above the Lazy Luncheonette.

As he awoke, his memory began to kick in. There had been a huge party at the Miner's Arms the previous night to celebrate coming out of the hostage situation alive. He vaguely recalled saying he would pay for a replacement *Pagliaccio* for Sheila, but the bulk of the night was lost in an alcohol induced fog.

Gemma and Vickers had come along late in the evening, bringing news of Ingleton.

"As you know he murdered five women in Sanford," Gemma began.

"Five?" Brenda had asked.

"Including Rosemary Ecclesfield," Vickers explained.

"What you don't know," Gemma said, picking up the reins again, "is that he also murdered his wife. She didn't leave at all. She's buried in a wood somewhere near Keighley. So he has that to face as well. He'll never come out."

"Lunatic," Joe had agreed, and gone back to partying.

He could not recall much more other than he had refused to let Sheila risk going home alone, but he was so drunk it was up to Brenda to organise a taxi for the three of them.

And now, here he was in a strange bedroom, in a strange bed, when he should be behind the counter of the Lazy Luncheonette.

And he was not alone, as he realised when the woman next

to him moved and groaned.

His mind was filled with images of Angela Foster. After George's report on her, Joe had invited her to the Miner's Arms, and he had passed some of the time chatting her up at the party.

He turned over, looked at her, then closed his eyes to go back to sleep. They opened again and he stared in shock. "Oh, no. Not you."

Brenda's eyes opened and she squinted to look at him. "Oh. Good morning, Joe… JOE!!!"

She leapt out of bed and clutched at her forehead. Joe dimly recalled that Brenda, too, had been quite drunk the previous night.

Realising she was wearing only a flimsy nightie, she snatched a gown from the door and wrapped herself in it.

"We dropped Sheila off," Joe said, "So what happened after that?"

"Oh, for God's sake, don't tell me…"

"Did we?" Joe asked. "I can't remember."

"Me neither, but…. Oh, dear Lord, this I terrible. I would never… not with you."

Joe clambered out of bed and with some embarrassment realised he was wearing only a pair of shorts. "I, er, I'd better get dressed."

He made hurriedly for the door.

As he opened it, Brenda stopped him. Wearing her meanest gaze, she warned him, "If you ever say one word of this to anyone, anyone at all, I will bury you alive. Understand?"

"My lips are sealed," he promised. "I have a reputation to maintain, too, you know. As far as anyone else is concerned, I don't remember anything about last night."

"Just make sure you keep up the pretence."

Joe smiled weakly. "Who's pretending?"

THE END

Fantastic Books
Great Authors

Meet our authors and discover our exciting range:

- Gripping Thrillers
- Cosy Mysteries
- Romantic Chick-Lit
- Fascinating Historicals
- Exciting Fantasy
- Young Adult and Children's Adventures

Visit us at:
www.crookedcatpublishing.com

Join us on facebook:
www.facebook.com/crookedcatpublishing

Printed in Great Britain
by Amazon.co.uk, Ltd.,
Marston Gate.